Tear Stained Beaches

COURTNEY GIARDINA

All Rights Reserved. Published in the United States by Take Two Publishing LLC, New Jersey.

www.taketwopublishing.com

ISBN: 978-0-9896533-2-9

Book Cover Design: Justin Giardina

Editing By: Dionne Lister

DEDICATION

To my family: Without you I would not be the strong, independent, determined woman I am today. You've stood beside me in all the moments that mattered most and taught me to never put a limit on my dreams.

To my amazing friends for believing in me on the days I don't believe in myself. And for always giving me the strength to stand back up each time I fall.

Preface

I'm not sure what it was that night. Lying in bed, tossing and turning, I wasn't able to sleep. My head was spinning with all sorts of thoughts, and my heart raced at the very thought that any one of them could be true. He had been texting often lately; much more than ever before. His phone never seemed to leave his side, and you could see the panic on his face every time it was within my grasp. His business trips became more frequent. Yes, work was busy, but how often does a lawyer need to travel when they're only licensed to practice in one state?

I kept telling myself that I was being paranoid, that he wasn't like my exes. After all, he wasn't the high school boyfriend who shattered my heart into pieces; he was my husband of five years. The most trusting man I had ever met. There's no way the man who proposed in a quaint little bed and breakfast, after drawing me a bath and ordering in room service, would do anything to intentionally hurt me. I must have been crazy to think that.

I tried my best to smile and drew the covers up to my chin, telling myself to relax. He was just a dedicated working-man. A man who worked hard for the house we had, the life we lived, and the luxury cars that sat in the driveway.

I closed my eyes, and our Jamaican honeymoon came to life.

1

What an amazing time we had that week. It rained for most of it, but those were the best parts. No one was hogging the Jacuzzi when it was pouring, so we saw our chance and took it. Hell, we were wet anyway, so the rain didn't bother us. I actually found it romantic. Every evening, at sunset, we headed down to the deserted end of the beach and took pictures of the starfish that hung close to shore. The last memory before falling asleep was of myself: bright orange starfish in hand, turning my head toward the camera, smiling and in love. It was almost two in the morning when I woke to the door squeaking open. I kept my eyes closed, listening to him move around in the darkness. After a few moments, he lifted the covers to crawl in. He edged closer to me and wrapped his arm around my waist. I took a deep breath and paused. My eyes shot open as a tear slowly rolled down my cheek. I stared straight ahead, careful not to move and betray that I was awake. A shiver ran up my arm where his hand rested. I lay there, staring into space, my gaze lingering almost as intensely as the smell of her perfume.

Chapter 1

I let the tear fall onto my pillow. He'd never come home with the smell of perfume before. Nor had he ever been out past midnight. Where could he have possibly been until two in the morning? I refused to move; I couldn't let him see me like this. There was no way I could explain myself, and throwing around accusations when I had nothing to back it up seemed useless. I listened to the clock tick for what seemed like hours. Actually, I'm pretty sure it was. I was making myself sick just thinking about what he would say in the morning. Was he really out with just a friend? Or was there another woman? What did she look like, and did she know about me? Was she taller than me, skinnier than me, prettier than me? My head was spinning. This was not happening. There's no way that my husband was having an affair. He knew how strongly I felt about adultery. The mere thought of it made my skin crawl.

I told myself I was being ridiculous, that I was overreacting. But now—I didn't know anything anymore. Never before had I woken in the middle of the night to roll over and find my husband not there, only to have him stumble home in the early morning hours. The second hand seemed to move slower and slower. Every time I thought I'd actually been able to sleep, I'd look at the clock and not even five minutes would have passed. I lay there, wide-awake, in his arms, praying quietly that my intuition was just out of whack. It was every wife's worst nightmare. The one thing they all fear, and it was possible I was living in the middle of it.

I'm not sure what time it was when I finally fell asleep, but I jumped up at 7 a.m. at the sound of the alarm clock. He slowly unwrapped his arm from around me and reached over to turn it off. Even with his lack of a full-night's sleep, Chase had no problem waking up. I, on the other hand, was completely exhausted. My eyes were so heavy; I kept them closed for as long as I could. Begging for just a few extra seconds of the sleep I'd lost.

"Good morning beautiful," he said.

I rolled over onto my back and smiled. When I finally opened my eyes, his were looking back at me. I wanted to cry. Thinking of those eyes looking at anyone else the way they looked at me broke my heart. He kissed my forehead and rolled out of bed, grabbing his cell phone from the night stand before heading into the bathroom to get ready.

"Late night, huh?" I asked.

"Very late, sorry about that. Alex called me when I was finished with my meeting. Said he needed to talk. I guess he's having some trouble at home. So we went out to Happy Jack's for a couple drinks and just got carried away. I hope I didn't wake you."

"I think I heard your car pull in, but must have fallen asleep before you even came in," I lied.

4

I tried to push all the awful thoughts to the back of my mind. After all, it is possible there was a simple answer to the perfume, and he really could have gotten caught up in an innocent conversation with a friend. I know it's happened to me when I've gone out with my girlfriends. Time just gets away from you. At least that's what I kept telling myself as I watched him button up his blue striped shirt and khaki shorts.

"Going golfing, I presume?"

"You know me so well." He laughed as he walked over, leaned in, and kissed me goodbye. I watched him walk out the door.

There was no way I was going back to bed, so I headed to the kitchen to make some breakfast. I pulled the frying pan out of the cupboard under the island and lit up the gas cook-top to make an omelet. Once the eggs started to cook, my mind wandered. I could see her vividly; a ghost made real by my insecurity. She was blond, tall, with hazel eyes. Then, my height, about 5'3" with the same short, curly brown hair I had. It wasn't that I thought I wasn't attractive enough for Chase, but if he was really having an affair, there must be something I was lacking. Maybe she liked to talk about football or cars. Maybe she could make him laugh more than I did. Was she better in bed? I probably could've driven myself crazy thinking of scenarios. My poor omelet received the brunt of my frustration as these thoughts pummeled my mind. I used the spatula to poke it to death. It didn't really matter anyway; at that point I had lost my appetite. I banged the frying pan on the side of the trash can and let the eggs fall in.

There was only one thing in life that could calm me down in moments like this: running. I used the alone time on the open road to clear my head. Now seemed like a good time to find some tranquility, so I dressed in my workout gear and headed out the door. The music on my iPhone was turned up, but I couldn't drown out the horrible thoughts that screamed in my head. I ran fast, pushed hard. Not because I was running towards anything; I was running away. Away from a life that had become so intertwined with doubt that I didn't know what truth I could hold onto anymore. I felt the sun graze my face as I sped further and further from it all. The only negative part about running was that at some point I knew I'd have to stop. I'd have to turn around and go back. And whatever troubles had haunted me when I left, would be waiting upon my return.

Chapter 2

It was a Monday morning the first time I saw his face. It was a moment that never faded over the years. I remember it well because it wasn't the grandest first impression a girl could've made, but at least it was a memorable one.

Slaving away at a local coffee shop in Copper Grove, NC wasn't the ideal way I wanted to spend my time, but it was the most convenient job I could find as I finished up my senior year at Schroeder University. At least my friend and co-worker Jessica helped me pass the time. That Monday, after the morning rush had died down, we took a break, sipped our café mochas behind the counter, and chatted about the exciting events of the past weekend. There was always some sort of drama in Jessica's love life, and I looked forward to all of her stories once the week began.

"Everywhere I turned, there he was. I couldn't escape him," Jessica said. "There was no way to leave the bar without him noticing, so I went to the bathroom and crawled out the window, mini dress, heels, and all."

I laughed.

"No laughing, it was not funny. I lost one of my heels and

spent at least 10 minutes searching around in the dark for it."

The story kept getting better. She brushed her silky, straight, black hair from her almond-shaped eyes each time she reached a suspenseful part. Before she could finish, her commentary was interrupted by the chiming of the bell at the front of the café.

I got to the register just in time to see a gorgeous, brown-haired guy in a dark blue button-up shirt walking in. His muscular arms and broad shoulders filled every inch of the sleeves. I looked up into grayish-blue eyes.

I stumbled over my words as I prepared to take his order. "Good morning, how can I have you, I mean help you today?"

"Can I get a large coffee with extra cream and a shot of espresso?" He smiled.

Once the order was entered into the register, I found myself lost in his eyes. I'm sure most guys would have been slightly freaked out by how intently I was staring, but if he was, he didn't show it.

"It's $3.75 right?" he asked, gently placing his black briefcase on the counter to gather the change.

"Yeah, right down to the penny. I guess you come here often?" I asked.

"Every Monday around this time." His deep voice sent shivers through my body.

I nodded my head, then turned away from him. "Hey Jessica, can you get me…"

I didn't even have to finish as Jessica hurriedly made her way over to the counter, drink in hand. She almost knocked me over as she reached out to him. Apparently, those same boyish good looks had distracted her just as much as they had me.

"Here you go Chase," she said.

That was when I first learned his name. Just as she set the drink on the counter, that's when it happened. I made a permanent mark on this fine-looking stranger.

"Exact change as always," he said, reaching his hand towards me.

As I reached out to grab it, my hand grazed his, and the calmness I had tried to exude since he'd walked through the door unraveled. I jerked my hand back. The change dropped to the counter and as I scrambled to pick it up, I knocked the freshly brewed cup of coffee on its side.

"Whoa, watch out!" Jessica yelled as she pulled me back.

Chase pulled his briefcase off the counter and Jessica frantically looked around for some towels. I, on the other hand, did nothing; I just stood there with my jaw dropped open, staring at the coffee that was dripping to the floor.

"Here, take some of these," Jessica said as she thrust a roll of paper towels into my chest.

My bad luck continued as I missed Jessica's handoff and ended up dropping the paper towels onto the floor as well. I reached down to pick them up, and on the way banged the back of my head on the counter.

"Ow!" I screamed and grabbed the back of head.

"Oh dear gosh girl, what is going on with you?" After Jessica made sure everyone had noticed the catastrophe, both she and Chase burst out laughing. I was horrified, but thankful at the same time that he didn't seem upset.

"Thanks guys, real nice. My new concussion and I will be over here preparing another cup of coffee while you two bask in my humiliation."

"Oh come on, you have to admit it was funny," Jessica yelled after me.

"Real funny," I said as I waved my hand at her.

It took only a moment to remake the order, and this time I made sure to step away as I carefully placed it on the counter.

"Will you be here every Monday?" Chase jokingly asked.

"Unfortunately for you, I will be."

"Don't worry, we all have bad days. And look," he said holding up his briefcase, "clean as a whistle."

"Glad to hear it."

"Well, I've got to get out of here. Thanks for an eventful morning." He winked at me. "Good to see you again, Jessica."

As the door closed behind him, Jessica turned and looked at me, inquiring with those eyes of hers just what in the world had happened.

"Wow, I really just did that, didn't I?" I asked, breaking the silence.

"Ha, yes you did. And in front of Chase, of all people."

I shrugged my shoulders. Until that incredibly embarrassing moment, I had never seen him before. And with eyes that blue and a body like that, I surely would have remembered him.

"What? You don't know Chase Julian? Everybody knows Chase Julian. He was captain of the soccer team. He's a first year law student." She paused, waiting for a light bulb to go off in my head. When it didn't, she continued, "He dated Morgan Harris all of last year."

Although I had known Morgan Harris, her dating life it seems I was completely unaware of. Morgan was a popular volleyball player around campus and model material. She stood at 5'8", with long, curly blond hair and legs every girl would give their life for. The surprising part was, she really was a nice person. Not the typical mean girl you'd picture. She did a lot of community charity events, helped fundraise for local school sports teams, and said hi with a smile to everyone she walked by. She was in my biology class sophomore year, and we did a couple of projects together.

"Never heard of him," I said, as Jessica went on to tell me how she had heard Chase was officially 'back' on the market. It was rumored that Morgan was offered a job in New York City this past summer, and they both decided the long distance just wasn't going to work.

"I wouldn't mind mending his broken heart. Even if it's just for one night," Jessica laughed.

"Jessica!"

"Alright, I'll let you have first crack at him."

I shot her a look and shook my head. I told her she was free to do with him whatever her heart desired. I was so not interested. At least that's what I kept telling myself. There was something about him I couldn't get out of my mind. Something Jessica definitely picked up on.

"Right, so the way your jaw dropped when he walked through the door was what?" she asked.

"It did not," I blushed. "Anyway, I'm nothing like Morgan Harris. I'm sure we have nothing in common." Yet, little did I know what the future held for me and the boy in the dark blue button-up shirt.

I find it funny that you could pass the same person on the street, in a store, or even in your neighborhood many times before actually meeting, thinking you've never seen them before; but when you are finally introduced, they seem to pop up everywhere. I saw Chase in the coffee shop bright and early every Monday (his visits were something I pretended I didn't look forward to), but when it came to seeing him anywhere else, even around campus, I had never seen him; at least not until I made a total fool of myself, again.

I was cutting it close to the start of my marketing research final. Trying to do my hair as I raced down the sidewalk, I looked down for a quick second to tie my ponytail and wham! Papers flew everywhere.

"I'm so sorry," I said, hurryingly gathering the scattered mess into a partially organized pile.

With my focus on picking up the papers, I hadn't paid attention to who it was I had run into. My hands froze at the sound of Chase's voice: "It's fine really, don't worry about it."

I stood, and there he was.

"Ah, you again. You certainly have a way of getting a guy's attention, don't you?" He said, as I handed him a not-so-neatly-stacked pile of papers.

My palms began to sweat and my legs were shaking. "I think you just happen to catch me at the worst times." I laughed out loud, hoping it masked my utter humiliation, and my obvious infatuation.

12

"I'm about to be late for my final exam of the semester."

"Well, then you better keep running, we wouldn't want you to miss that midterm now, would we?"

"Thanks. Chase, right?" He nodded. "Sorry again." I said, walking as fast as I could as I made my way to the business building of the campus. Before I had gone too far, I heard him call out.

"Hey, coffee girl." I turned around. "You know my name, but I don't know yours."

So, for the first time since our original meeting at the coffee shop, I officially introduced myself. "It's Haylie. Haylie Manning."

"Well, you have a good day, Haylie Manning," he said, as he waved from a distance.

"You too," I shouted after him. My heart was about to pound out of my chest. He was just as cute in those jeans and polo shirt as he was in business attire. Maybe even better looking. Any way you put it, I guess Jessica was right. He was gorgeous. I stood there, frozen for a minute until reality kicked in. I was so going to be late for my marketing final.

Chapter 3

We had come a long way from that day at the college campus. We fell in love, married, and now called Charlotte, NC home. Sure it hadn't been totally perfect, but nothing in life ever was. The move to Charlotte was a fast one and came as quite a surprise. It had caught me off guard the day Chase brought the idea home. It had been a long day of work for me, and I was just finishing preparing dinner when the door to our apartment flew open. He pranced in excitedly and I could tell he was eager to tell me something.

"Well, look at you," I smiled. "Someone obviously had a good day."

"I did, as a matter of fact. I went out to lunch with Jack, and he made me an interesting proposition."

Jack was one of the partners in the law firm Chase worked for in Copper Grove. He had seen great potential in Chase from the start. When Chase's internship was coming to an end, Jack didn't hesitate to offer him an associate position within the firm. Since then, Jack had taken Chase under his wing, preparing him for bigger and better things.

"I'm intrigued," I said. "Go on."

"Jack has a good friend working at a big law firm up in New

York. He said they just opened an office out in the Charlotte area and they're looking for some up-and-comers to train within the firm to eventually become partners down the line. I guess a few weeks ago Jack had thrown my name into the mix, and they want to make me an offer." His smile was stretched from ear to ear.

"In Charlotte? That's quite the drive for a daily commute."

He laughed. "I think it could be a great opportunity for us—a new start in a new place for us to grow into. It would be a great adventure to share."

"You want to move to Charlotte?" I wasn't very fond of the idea at first. "What about me? I can't just leave my job."

"Honey, this is a once in a lifetime opportunity. Do you know how hard it is to become partner in a law firm? I can't pass this up. I need you with me on this."

"And I am with you on this. You know I support you in everything you do, but I thought we were happy here. I like my job, our apartment, and our friends."

I threw out every reason why we shouldn't move to Charlotte. Starting over was scary, and I was perfectly comfortable with the life we were living. I had just been promoted to Assistant Director of Marketing within the personal products company I worked for. A pretty good step up for someone just two years out of college, and I enjoyed the job. Chase and I had a routine that worked. Our life was very predictable.

It was that very word that made me finally understand Chase's thoughts. *Predictable.* In other words, boring. I thought back to our routine. Sure it worked for us, and yes we were happy, but exciting was not a word I would've used to describe our lives. I think Chase really wanted the excitement, the adventure that Charlotte was offering. I went over and over it in my mind after that conversation. Trying to figure out if it was the best thing for me, for Chase, and most of all, for us. It wasn't an easy to decision to make, but when it came down to it, I knew what decision was best. Life in Copper Grove would eventually hit a glass ceiling for Chase. One I knew we both would regret in the long run, and I didn't want it to cause any resentment when it did. It was time to think not only about myself, but my family. The one I had and the one I'd hoped someday to grow. With that, Chase and I packed up our memories in eastern North Carolina and headed west.

Chapter 4

Our first few months in Charlotte were a little rocky, as it took me a while to settle into our new life. It was frustrating not being able to find a job. I took my frustration out on Chase. I wanted to be the supporting wife I promised I would be, but I felt like I was losing a little bit of who I was. I had worked my way up in Copper Grove, and it was hard to leave, knowing I'd come to Charlotte with nothing lined up. As the understanding and mellow guy that Chase was, he always overlooked my grumpiness and assured me that, in time, I would find my place in this city as well. Moping around feeling sorry for myself wasn't getting me anywhere, so after a ton of searching and unsuccessful job interviews, I finally landed a part-time job as a Special Events Manager at a local country club. It wasn't the big, corner-office sort of job I had hoped for, but I enjoyed it more than I thought I would. Coordinating weddings, business meetings, private family parties, and charity events made up my job responsibilities.

After awhile, once I settled back into a normal work routine, I became much more pleasant to be around, and Chase and I were back to the happily-married couple we had moved there as.

We had lived in an apartment for most of our first year, before we came across our current home in a quiet little cul-de-sac in the small town of Oak Creek. It was an upscale neighborhood, and everyone was very friendly. Being just thirty minutes outside the Charlotte city center, it was a convenient commute for Chase and we had easy access to enjoy city life when we so desired.

Once we closed on our new home, Chase and I immediately got busy making it our own. We spent most weekends painting, decorating, and furniture shopping. I couldn't believe how involved he wanted to be with it all. We'd come home with loads of paint swatches, a different color palette every weekend, and Chase would tape them up on the walls of every room, trying to figure out which color would be best. Once we finally decided, we spent many nights after work dressed in old clothes, paint-brushes and rollers in hand, making it all come alive.

It took awhile, but after the painting was done and furniture was in the right places, we started to feel at home. We'd watch movies every Friday night, and enjoyed sipping wine via candlelight while taking a bubble bath in our new Jacuzzi tub. We couldn't have asked for anything more.

Two years after we moved to Charlotte, Chase's career began to thrive. Summer was just around the corner and he'd been working hard to prove his worth within the firm. He was really making a name for himself. I could tell, though, that it was taking its toll. At first, he brought home his extensive paperwork. He'd spend hours in the office, sorting through documents and preparing for each case. I put on my understanding and sympathetic wife hat, and before I headed up to bed I'd bring him a coffee to help him get through it.

"Here you go, an extra shot of espresso—just how you like it."

He grabbed the cup without looking up. "Thanks."

"How's it going?" I asked, trying to make conversation.

"It's eleven o'clock at night and I'm not even halfway through this pile of papers. How do you think it's going?" He snapped.

"Right, sorry. I met another one of the neighbors today; the one across the street. I think her name was Beverly. She seems really sweet."

"Haylie, I really have to get this stuff done. Can we talk about that later?"

"Sure. It's not important anyway. I'll see you upstairs." I kissed him on the forehead and left him to finish his paperwork.

I was saddened by the gradual shift in my husband's personality. The happy-go-lucky man that was always calming me down and assuring me things would be okay had suddenly turned into someone I had never seen before. We started to fight about everything. We'd fight about everything: him forgetting an event we RSVPed to, how, during his free time, he'd rather go out for a beer with his friends than spend time with his wife, and even whether or not it was supposed to rain that day. Little things turned into big arguments, and the dynamic between us had changed. We weren't agreeing on anything, we weren't communicating and, truthfully, neither of us thought the other was very pleasant to be around.

I begged him to take some time off of work, which at first he refused. I knew we couldn't live like this much longer. Being under the same roof was becoming unbearable. I wasn't sure how much more I could take.

"You need a break, Chase. You don't sleep, all you do is work, and you're starting to treat me like I'm the enemy."

"I'm under a lot of pressure, Haylie. This house doesn't pay for itself, you know."

"I never said it did." I tried not to raise my voice, but he made it very hard. "Do you see what I'm talking about? You twist all my words around." I continued to declare to him that I was not the bad guy. That if he continued to work like this, he was going to go over the edge. After much pleading, he finally agreed to take some time off. I think he finally understood the urgency of it.

"My friend Greg keeps bugging me to find some time for him. Maybe I'll give him a call and take him up on his offer."

Greg was an old college buddy of Chase's. They'd spent most of their college career attached at the hip and many spring breaks getting drunk together in Miami, New Orleans, or some other spring break hot spot. I liked Greg; he was a good guy. Chase hadn't seen him since graduation when Greg took a job in Virginia.

Chase contacted Greg and a vacation was arranged. He was thrilled to get away, just the two of them, and do normal guy stuff. Thankfully, over the next couple of weeks, knowing the vacation was coming, Chase lightened up. He apologized many times for his erratic behavior, and frequently came home with a bouquet of flowers to make sure I knew he meant it.

I kissed Chase goodbye as he leaned on the driver-side door of his car.

"Have fun, and no thinking about work." He didn't respond. "Promise?" I added in my cute-little-kid voice he always loved.

"I promise." He gave me one final kiss on the tip of my nose and disappeared into the driver's seat.

I was going to miss him for four whole days, but I knew we needed this time apart. I waved as he pulled out of the driveway. I turned around and spotted a familiar face sitting on the front porch next door.

"Hey there girlfriend!" It was Katie, my sweet and friendly neighbor.

"Beautiful night for a good book and Vino, huh?" she asked. She often sat out there on the nights her husband, Dave, worked late. He and Katie had been married about ten years and they seemed to have a pretty solid relationship. He was CEO of a large financial company and was away more often than not. The only time I saw him was when he was throwing his suitcase in his trunk and heading out for another long weekend away from home.

I loved Katie; she was the nicest out of all the wives in the neighborhood, and probably the most down to earth. When we first moved here, she greeted us with a homemade apple pie. She introduced me to the rest of the wives in the neighborhood and talked me into attending their regular Saturday gatherings. At first I was apprehensive. Although they were all very nice, it was hard at first to fit in with them. They were always so prim and proper—never stepped out of the house without their hair done and make-up on. They spent most of their days getting manicures, going to yoga, and shopping for shoes. They thought it was funny that I worked while my husband clearly brought home enough money to support the both of us. It really was the epitome of *Stepford Wives*, but like I said, they really were very nice. They just didn't understand my need to establish a career, feel accomplished in my professional life, and be able to help contribute financially. Needless to say, Saturday get-togethers were always interesting and unpredictable.

"Couldn't be a more perfect night!" I agreed.

"I have plenty in the wine cellar if you'd like to come over. Looks like you could use the company just as much as I could tonight." Knowing she was right, I accepted the invitation.

"Let me go wash up and change into something comfy, and I'll be right over."

The wind sent a slight chill through the air, so I wrapped myself in my zip-up hoodie and got comfortable next to Katie on the wicker bench that sat on her front porch. Before I could say a word, she popped open the cork on her Kendall-Jackson Chardonnay and poured me a glass.

"Spill it girl." She handed me a glass. She could read me like an open book and always knew when there was something going on— good or bad. I tried to deny what was obviously clear to Katie, but she didn't buy it. She assured me I'd feel better if I talked to someone about it, and, of course, who better to talk to than her?

It wasn't an easy subject to bring up. Admitting my marriage was less than perfect after all these years was tough. I chugged the glass of chardonnay and had started on my second one before I said a word. It gave me a moment to think about how exactly I was going to explain it. I guess it was simple, really. We had hit a bump in the road. Life had taken its toll. Filling her in on Chase's short temper, late night paperwork, and the lack of intimacy in the relationship poured out of my mouth a lot easier once the wine had kicked in. After putting it all out there, I asked Katie what her secret was. Dave was always hard at work, both in and out of state, and they seemed to have it all together. I wondered how they dealt with the stress of the job, managed time together, and how she helped him when things got overwhelming for him. It just seemed like everyone else had a handle on their lives. I was frustrated.

"First of all, you have to remember, things on the inside are not always what they seem on the outside." I wasn't sure what she meant by that, but she continued. She assured me that no relationship was perfect, and even though it may look that way, it was highly unlikely. She told me that no woman would directly come out and say they think their husband isn't attracted to them anymore or their husband doesn't pay attention to them. It's just second nature to mask problems by putting on their happy face for the world to see.

"Trust me; everyone goes through a rough patch. You two will get through it." She placed her hand on my shoulder and laughed at the fact that my second glass of wine seemed to have disappeared faster than my first. "Good thing you don't have far to go tonight."

It felt really good to be able to talk about all that was going on. Keeping it bottled up was driving me crazy. My worries had disappeared (for the time being) by the time we called it a night. I hugged Katie goodbye and thanked her for lending such a supportive ear. It was just after midnight and my head was certainly spinning by the time I stumbled the 100 yards home and crawled into bed.

Chapter 5

It was a little after nine on Monday night when I heard the familiar sound of a car heading down the street. Chase was finally home. I couldn't wait to hear all about his trip with Greg, and silently prayed that he'd be back to his normal self again after a nice, rejuvenating vacation. I was so excited for him to come into the house. I had really missed him.

"Hey there." I squealed excitedly as I saw his head peek through the front door. He smiled at me as I went over and hugged him. I noticed almost immediately that something was off. The way he held me, it was different. Maybe I was just expecting more, but I was saddened at the thought that surely Chase was not back to his usual self at all.

I asked him all sorts of questions about his trip and although he answered each and every one, he didn't seem too excited about any of it. He didn't go into detail about much, and after a while changed the subject.

"How about you? What did you do while I was gone?" I told him I'd spent most of the weekend with Katie. Then did the normal weekend things: went for a run, picked up some groceries at the farmers market, and even did a little gardening. "Sounds like you had a good time."

I headed up to bed while Chase prepared his briefcase for his return to work in the morning. I made my normal rounds of washing my face, brushing my teeth, and turning down the bed, before sliding out of my jeans and t-shirt and searching through my pajama drawer for something to wear.

Suddenly I felt a breath of hot air on my neck. I could feel the hairs stand up. I turned around and Chase pulled me in close. He kissed me, as if he had something to prove—I'm not sure if it was to me or himself.

We made love that night, but I could feel the distance between us. Something just wasn't the same. Physically he was there with me, lips touching mine, body up against me, but his mind— I could tell it was somewhere else. I thought back to the very first time we made love. It was nothing like this moment.

We had been dating about six months. I was officially a college graduate, and Chase was in his second year of law school. One night, after a stressful day at work, I headed over to Chase's. I wasn't planning on it as I was tired and frustrated, but he insisted. During my lunch break we had spoken, and he could tell something was wrong. He tried his best to cheer me up over the phone, and I admired him for that. Even at my worst, he always knew how to put a smile on my face.

"What is this?" I asked, as I made my way into his apartment.

"I thought you could use a little cheering up."

The lights were dimmed. My path to the table was a candle-lit sea of rose petals. Dinner waited.

"Cheese ravioli. Your favorite," he smiled.

He wrapped me in his arms and my day of stress was already fading into the distance. That was the night I knew he was a keeper. A man who brought out the best in me was all I had ever needed.

After dinner we cuddled on the couch for a bit. It was late and I was too tired to drive back to my place. I had an early start at work the next morning, so before I had the chance to fall asleep on the couch, I got up to shower and get ready for bed. I let the hot water run down my back and wash away the stress of the day.

After the shower, I wrapped a towel around me and brushed my teeth. On nights I spent at Chase's, I always borrowed one of his t-shirts to sleep in. I walked into the bedroom to rummage through his drawer and as I bent over to look for a shirt, I felt his hands slide across my waist. He leaned over me and kissed the back of my neck. I smiled and closed my eyes.

"You really are something special, you know that?" He stood me up.

"I could say the same for you," I said, as I turned towards him.

He gently pulled me in closer. Our lips met, as we savored each other. He made his way to my neck and I could feel my heart racing. He stopped for a moment and stared at me, waiting for a sign that this was alright. I grabbed his white t-shirt and slowly slid it up out of his jeans, past his incredibly defined abs, to his chest. He lifted his arms up, and I pulled it over his head. That was all the sign he needed. He un-tucked my towel and let it fall to the floor. He wrapped his arms around my waist and lifted me gently from the floor. He lay me down on the bed and hovered over me. There I was: naked, vulnerable, and yet completely comfortable with this man staring at every part of me. I could hear his belt unbuckle and the rustle of his jeans as they hit the floor.

His body was warm as it touched mine. My hands brushed up and down his back as he kissed me and made his way inside. My hands grasped tightly at his skin. I felt his soft lips against my neck and my back arched at the sensation overcoming me.

The sex was amazing that night, and every time after that, and there certainly wasn't any lack of it. We had always had a great passion for each other. On top of that passion, as time went on, we fell more and more in love.

Tonight, that passion was gone. When we were finished, I rested my head on his chest. Instead of the happy fulfillment I used to feel, I was filled with sadness. I couldn't understand why things were so difficult lately, why we couldn't seem to get our marriage back on track.

Chapter 6

That night was only the beginning. As the weeks went on, I was spending many dinner date nights by myself. I'd stare a while at the empty plate on the other end of the table, before I finally called it a night. At first, both dinners would get cold before I'd even think of touching mine. Then slowly, the time I'd wait became less and less.

I fell asleep alone most nights, as late-night work meetings kept him out into the post-midnight hours. I tried not to let it get to me, as I knew Chase was working very hard to try and make partner. He certainly deserved it, and I had tried everything I could to be the supportive wife he needed me to be. I let the excuses slide, but there soon became more and more of them. *Sorry honey, my meeting ran late. I won't be home for dinner tonight; I'm meeting with a client across town. Can we reschedule our date tonight? I have to finish some paperwork at the office.*

It wasn't until a couple of months later, when Chase went off to Chicago with a few of the lawyers from his firm that my suspicions increased. He told me that he and some of the guys had decided to get out of their element in hopes of getting something accomplished. He was gone only a few days and would call me at the same time every night. At exactly 9 p.m. my phone would ring.

"Hey babe, how was your day?" he asked.

"Oh the usual. Nothing too exciting here. How is Chicago?"

"It's definitely windy; that's for sure. Been great though."

"Tell me more. What did you do today?"

"Listen babe, I'd love to talk more, but I don't really have the best service here. You're cutting out kind of bad."

"Oh alright. Well, have a good night honey. Love you."

"You too. I'll call you tomorrow."

He hung up the phone. I tried to ignore my fears. Even though he had been absent lately, I'd seen nothing that would make me doubt he was telling the truth. He'd never done anything in the past to give me reason to believe anything other than he was on a business trip with a bunch of guys from work. That was, until I ran into his colleague Jay at the grocery store the day before Chase was scheduled to return. I waved at him from a distance. He made his way over to the produce section, where I had begun to frivolously search for the perfect bunch of bananas.

"Hey Haylie, what's going on?" Jay asked.

"Oh you know. The usual weekly grocery trip. How about you? Do anything exciting this weekend?"

"Just brought the kids to the park. Trying to teach Emma how to ride a bike. Had her head-to-toe in protective gear, and she still gets hurt," he laughed.

Chuckling at the thought of it I replied, "Gotta love kids. Well, tell Helen I said hi and have a great rest of the weekend." My smile was forced. His weekend activities clearly didn't include Chicago. I tossed the bananas in my cart and went on my way.

I never mentioned that encounter to Chase, but when he came

home the next day I tried to nonchalantly get out of him who had accompanied him on the trip.

He was vague, and never said anyone's name. Just told me it was the usual group of guys. I didn't necessarily think, at that point, it was another woman, but I did worry that Chase was getting tired of me, that for some reason he just didn't want to be around me anymore.

Chapter 7

I promised myself that when Chase got home from Chicago I was going to really try and put our marriage back together. We just didn't seem to be connecting anymore, and I was determined to fix it. I wanted him to be attracted to me again, to want to spend time with me and rekindle the flame that had dimmed over time. I had planned, for the following Friday night, the date night we'd neglected for so long.

Work went by faster than I thought it would. I called our favorite Chinese restaurant. I went by and picked up our order on the way home. Chase's silver Mercedes wasn't in the driveway when I pulled up, so I assumed he was running late, again. When I got out, I could see Katie in her usual spot on her front porch. I gave a quick wave as I hurried towards the front door. I hope she'd get the hint I wasn't in the mood for a neighborly conversation tonight. I wanted to make sure everything was perfect for Chase's arrival.

I set out the Chinese food on the coffee table in the living room. The one thing Chase and I always found enjoyable was the way we always ate our meals on movie nights. We cuddled on the couch in the living room, plates in front of us with our movie of choice on the flat screen that hung over the gas fireplace. That was something we hadn't done in about two or three months. He was rarely home for dinner, and if he was, it was usually after I got tired of waiting for him. I was almost afraid that tonight wasn't going to be any different, but just as I was about to sit down and search through the list of current movies-on-demand, familiar headlights flashed through the kitchen window.

He sat in the car for some time after the engine died. I pulled the curtain in the living room back just enough to see through to the driveway. He was on the phone, laughing and smiling, which was unusual for a business call. I'd seen plenty of those. His face was emotionless, stern as could be, when talking to clients. He had always told me a poker face was much needed in his line of work. Once you got emotionally involved, you were of no use to your client. It was about ten minutes later when he finally walked in the door.

He kissed me on the forehead as he breezed by. "Hey babe, sorry I'm late. I'm a little behind at the office, had to catch up. What's for dinner?"

"I got your favorite. Sesame chicken, lo mein, and crab rangoons from Yeung Chi. Thought it might be a good way to end a stressful day."

"Sounds great, I'm just going to go wash up and change. I'll be fast."

"Ok, I'll order the movie while you're up there. Don't be long," I pleaded.

I wanted a night alone with my husband. I'd been longing for him to hold me, to just be with me, to try. I needed reassurance. Chase was a huge Adam Sandler fan and so I ordered *Just Go With It*. I thought it would be the perfect choice for a night like tonight.

Chase was quick in the shower; he came back down in his gray flannel pajamas and a solid navy t-shirt. He sat right next to me on the couch, the food was all set out and the movie just waiting to be played. He put his left arm around me and pulled me in closer as he grabbed his fork. I hit play and our romantic night began.

It was off to a good start, for about a half hour into the movie. Dinner was put away and Chase and I had laughed simultaneously at every other scene. At that point, Chase had laid us both down on the couch. He put his arm around me as I rested my head on the pillow. I almost forgot about all my concerns over the last few days, as everything at that moment was perfect. Unfortunately, that moment didn't last long. It was abruptly interrupted.

Chase pulled the phone from his pocket. "Sorry babe, I'll turn off the ringer."

I rolled my eyes with the back of my head facing him. For the rest of the movie, Chase's phone must have gone off half a dozen times, if not more. Even though he had put it on silent, I could still here the sounds of his fingers pushing the keys. I couldn't see his face, nor could I see the cell phone, but I was greatly annoyed that he chose not to ignore whoever it was for another hour while he spent time with his wife.

"Really, Chase?" I finally said with a scowl.

"What?" he asked.

I turned around and glared at him. "Are you even paying any attention at all to the movie?"

"Yes I'm paying attention. What's with the attitude?"

"You have been on your phone for the last half hour. Don't

think I don't notice just because I have my back to you."

"Haylie, calm…" He started to speak, but I interrupted.

"No, I will not calm down. This is supposed to be our night. We haven't spent a night alone together in so long and you have to ruin it by texting. I mean, who could you possibly be talking to?"

"Oh Haylie, really? What are you trying to get at now?"

It really was a waste of my breath. I knew that. No matter what the situation, I was always the crazy one. The one who overreacted and made something out of nothing. So with his last comment, I fought the urge to retaliate and rolled back over towards the flat screen.

I felt him squirm behind me as he placed the phone back in his pocket. "Look, I'm putting the phone away now, okay? My attention is one hundred percent on you."

I didn't answer; just lay quietly watching the movie. I had tried so hard, but to no avail. Chase continued to drift further and further away from me.

Chapter 8

Moments like that continued for the next couple of months. Chase would come home and sit in the car for about 10-15 minutes with the phone to his ear. When he did finally come inside, he would text until the time he went to bed. The only time that phone ever left his hand was when he'd jump in the shower before bed. And even then, he'd bring it into the bathroom with him and set it on the countertop. Sometimes I would make a snide remark about how ridiculous it was that his phone never left his hands. Chase would get angry, call me crazy, and ignore me the rest of the night.

One night, on a rare occasion he was home for dinner, the ringing phone interrupted us. At first he ignored it, but when it rang for a third time, he excused himself from the table and went outside. Of course, being paranoid, I tip-toed to the front window to see what I could hear. No part of the conversation came out clear, as he was standing too far off the front porch, but I swear I could hear the voice on the other end of the line. As he turned to walk back up the porch, the voice became clearer. It was a woman's voice; there was no mistaking it.

I hurried back to the dining room table before he'd notice I was spying, and sat down. By the time he'd walked back in, I had thrown a bite of food in my mouth. I stared at him, and waited for him to share his conversation. He didn't look up; he just looked at his plate, and cut his chicken into the perfectly even pieces he needed before he would take a bite.

I rolled my eyes and stabbed my fork into the grilled chicken on my plate and then asked, "Important phone call?"

"No. Just Alex making sure we were still on for tomorrow."

Alex was one of the husbands in our cul-de-sac. He was married to a petite brunette named Allison. This was her second marriage. She was thirty-four and he just twenty-five. They found out they were having their first child about six months into their relationship. Alex proposed just a few months later, and they had married in a small garden ceremony two months before Allison welcomed baby Austin into the world. They had a little girl named Madelyn a year later.

Alex had started coming around more and more lately, as apparently he realized—a little too late—that he wasn't ready for the whole kid thing just yet. He needed time away and would ask Chase to head to the local pub for a beer. He was also Chase's main workout buddy. Every weekend they made it a point to hit the gym in the mornings before doing anything else.

I knew better. The voice on the other end of the line was not Alex. I knew contradicting him would just end in another fight. Lately, that phone seemed to be the core of all of my anxiety, but I didn't say a word.

We went to bed that night like nothing happened, and the next morning I woke up to an empty bed. Chase was already at the gym with Alex by the time I awoke. It was my one Saturday of the month I had to work at the country club; but with all the stress I'd been under, I had woken before my alarm had gone off.

I distracted myself with housework for the next hour, trying to ignore the fact that Chase hadn't even woke me up to kiss me goodbye. I vacuumed all the bedrooms, dusted the dressers, mopped the tile floors and threw in a few loads of laundry. I rearranged the furniture on our wrap-around front porch, and sat down to pay some bills that were due the next week. By that time, I had to get ready for work.

All day, I kept thinking about the voice on the other end of the line. Who could Chase have been talking to, and why was it so important for him to lie about it? Was he really capable of cheating on me? His secrets, distance, and excuses had begun to set in, and my paranoia had officially begun. I checked my phone regularly, but didn't hear from Chase all day. When it was time for me to lock up and head home, I called to see where he was; but no answer. This was not the kind of life I thought I would be living. My marriage was failing and it was the worst feeling in the world.

"Dammit." In the midst of repeatedly dialing Chase's number, I dropped my purse onto the pavement and all the contents scattered over the ground. I shoved everything back in and walked to the car. The car shook when I slammed the door. I jammed the key in the ignition and stomped on the accelerator.

After arriving home, I called Chase a few more times, with no success. Finally, just as I was about to relax in a bubble bath, my phone rang. I picked it up.

"It's about time."

"Hi babe, sorry I missed your calls earlier, but I don't really have service in here."

"Where are you?" I demanded.

"Alex and I decided to go out for a few beers in the city. I hope that's okay. I won't be home too late."

I shook my head in disbelief. I felt hopeless and was tired of always being angry. I didn't argue about his boys night out, I just hung up the phone and poured a tall glass of wine. I sank into the bubbles of the Jacuzzi tub and let the warm water relieve the tension that had built up in my muscles. The name Alex was really starting to get on my nerves.

I tried to relax and drown my sorrows by blaring Nick Lachey's *What's Left of Me* CD. Even the lavender bath oils couldn't calm me. After awhile, my eyes grew heavy. I drained the tub and dressed for bed. Sleep was a while in coming, but when I succumbed, it was deep and blissfully numbing.

Chapter 9

Later that week, after missing another one of our planned dinners, Chase returned home late. I was in the kitchen loading the dishwasher when he came in. I didn't have to say a word.

"I know, I know, late again. I'm sorry baby, but you know I can't help it."

He slid his hands around my waist and kissed the tip of my ear. I pulled away abruptly as I pulled the dishes from the sink.

"Alright, well it's been a long day. I'll see you in bed." He squeezed me a little tighter before he let go and headed upstairs.

After finishing my evening chores, I made my way upstairs. I slipped into my pajamas and headed into the bathroom to brush my teeth. Just then, I saw Chase's phone light up. I had tried on multiple occasions to take a peek at his phone when he was in the shower. I told myself it was just to ease my mind and confirm that all the worrying was for nothing. To my surprise, he had password protected it and I couldn't get in. It never stopped me from trying, though I had no success. This time, however, I didn't even have to try. I looked down at his phone, just in time to see a text come through. It quickly scrolled across the screen, but I caught all of it.

Counting down the days, I'll call you when I get out.

Counting down the days to what? I didn't remember Chase telling me about any event coming up; if he had, I would have put it on the calendar. The number wasn't assigned to a contact, but the area code was not a local Carolina number, and that's what caught my eye. Once the phone went black, I could no longer access it without the password, so I made sure not to forget the area code.

Turning into a completely senseless human being, I returned downstairs to my laptop, logged into our joint cell phone account and pulled up the phone call records. First, I clicked on incoming/outgoing calls and searched for the area code. At first, it showed up just a few times, but as I clicked the pages to the most recent dates, the number of times seemed to increase dramatically. He had called that number every night over the last two weeks on his way home from work. It was the last call he would make before he came into the house for the night and the first call he made when he left for work in the morning.

Clearly this person was important to Chase and I was anxious to figure out whose number this was. Once I clicked on the text message report, I had to look twice at the number of texts exchanged on his phone. In just two weeks, he had exchanged 2800 text messages. As I scrolled down the screen, it was obvious at least three quarters of those were back and forth to this number.

"Babe, I'm going to hit the hay, I've got an early Saturday morning workout planned with Alex. You coming up anytime soon?" I jumped a good two feet off the couch, flinging the laptop in the air.

"Uh, yeah. I just want to clean up some things down here.

Don't wait up, I'll be in soon."

"Alright. Goodnight, beautiful."

I shivered. Did he think I was stupid? The sooner I found out what was going on, the better off I'd be in the long-run.

I sat downstairs until I no longer heard him rustling around in the bedroom. I wanted to make sure he was in bed before I made my way into his office. I wasn't sure what I was going to do, but I needed more information. I knew something was wrong; something was going on and I refused to be played for a fool.

I rifled through all of his drawers, my hands shaking as they sorted through papers, pushing things from side to side, trying to find something; anything. I pulled out invoices for work, airport-parking receipts, and then I came upon a current credit card statement.

5/1/11 - Relaxation Spa- Charleston, SC, $165.00
6/8/11 - 1-800 Flowers, $77.50
7/12/11 - Bistro 491- Augusta, GA, $110.89
8/1/11 - Kay Jewelers- Charlotte, NC, $1250.61

Bile rose to my mouth. I never got any spa treatment, let alone in Charleston, and I certainly didn't remember any flowers delivered or jewelry gifts given. I also never remembered Chase talking about making any sort of trip Georgia. Where the hell was I? My accusations were holding more water, but I had nothing concrete he wouldn't try to lie his way out of. I made a copy of the credit card statement, willing the copier to go faster, and tucked the page into my purse. I was meeting with the girls tomorrow morning and was planning on telling them about my suspicions.

It's funny how everything you find out, no matter how close it is staring you in the face, you will hold on to the denial until the very end, until you no longer have a choice and the lies have nowhere left to hide. I made sure everything was back where I found it; I turned off the lights, and headed up to bed to a man I wasn't sure I knew anymore.

Chapter 10

It was Saturday morning, and it was time to brave breakfast with the girls at Beverly's house. Beverly thought that having a close-knit community was important; so even though attending was optional, everyone felt compelled to go.

Beverly was like the ringleader of the group. She organized all neighborhood parties, tried her hardest to get everyone to march to the beat of her drum, and always had to make sure she knew what was going on in everyone's life. She was the one who'd been in the neighborhood the longest. Unlike the other houses that had switched hands a few times before we all finally settled in, Beverly and her husband Mike had built theirs from the ground up.

Beverly greeted me at the door with a high-pitched squeal of excitement. "Haylie, so happy you could make it."

"Always a pleasure, Beverly." It took every ounce of energy I could muster to fake a smile.

She escorted me into the sunroom, where the rest of the girls had gathered. My desire to tell everyone about my problems was waning, and I barely heard the conversations chattering on around me.

I guess my nerves were quite obvious as Katie questioned my demeanor. "Hayles? Are you okay?" I didn't answer right away, as I was still searching for the right words. "If something is bothering you, girl, you know you can tell us."

I didn't know where to start, so I just blurted out, "I think Chase is having an affair."

Beverly gasped as she placed her hand on her chest. "Oh, I'm so sorry honey."

"I've been suspecting it for quite a while. Things just haven't been right. And last night, well, I found this."

I pulled the piece of paper out of my purse and showed them the credit card statements. They had all been so nice to me over the years; and despite our differences, I was looking forward to their support. I really needed them right then. Beverly looked at me and took my hand.

"Honey, I'm so glad you came to us for this. We know exactly what you're going through. We're all here to help in any way we can."

"Thanks, Beverly. I'm really struggling with how to bring it up to him. I mean, do I just hand this to him and ask for an explanation?"

"Bring it up to him? Now why on earth would you do that?" She looked at me as if I had just asked if I should wear a pink blouse with a red skirt.

"What do you mean, why would I do that? What am I supposed to do?" I asked.

"Take it from a woman who knows. Take that piece of paper and throw it away. Forget you ever saw it and move on with your life. Am I right ladies?"

She looked around at our breakfast companions: they were all nodding. My heart hollowed as each woman turned against me.

"What do you mean, forget it?" I stood up and pulled my hand from hers.

"Haylie, do you know how many women would kill to be in our shoes? This kind of life comes at a price, and we all have to pay for it in some way. You have to learn to turn your head from these things."

Allison, Alex's wife, chimed in, "I know it may not be something you expected, but it will hurt you more to find out the truth. Trust me; I know Alex is not meeting with clients until all hours of the night on a weekly basis. It may sound foolish, but look at what he's given me: two wonderful kids, a roof over my head, and freedom to do whatever my heart desires. If I don't ask, he doesn't tell, and what I don't know won't hurt me."

"I'm sorry," my eyes were wide and I couldn't keep the anger out of my voice, "are you telling me that you know Alex is having an affair with another woman, and you're okay with it?"

Beverly leaned across and whispered to me, "*Women* would be the proper term, sweetie." If I'd had a glass cup in my hand at that point, glass would've shattered everywhere.

"Women? You mean there's been more than one?" The look on Allison's face confirmed it. "I don't even understand how you can be accepting of this. That is not what a marriage is supposed to be! A husband is supposed to love his wife and be loyal, honest, and caring."

"Haylie, calm down," Allison said. "Life doesn't always work out to be the fairytale we hoped for. Sometimes love dies, but that doesn't mean that Alex and I don't have mutual respect for each other; because we do."

"Okay, I really have to go." I threw my crumpled napkin onto

45

the table and snatched my purse from behind me.

"Haylie, please don't leave." If anyone could have gotten me to stay, it would've been Katie. But there was nothing she could say to me right then that would change my mind.

"A man who respects his wife does not sleep with other women. And a woman who respects herself does not allow her husband to get away with it." That was the last thing I said before I headed out the door.

I was more determined than ever to find out the truth. How could those women fully acknowledge that their husbands were having affairs and just go on being married to them? I was not going to let that happen to me. I moved away from a great job, family, and a town I loved so Chase could go after his dream. How dare he treat me like this. There was no way in hell I was going to live my life with a cheating husband. It was time to act.

Chapter 11

Chase was gone most of Saturday and didn't arrive home until bedtime. He had worked out with Alex; after that, they'd hit the golf course for their third weekend in a row, and then gone out for drinks. At least that's what he told me. Honestly, I didn't know anymore. What I did know was that I'd had enough of being treated this way, and it was time I'd talked to him about his inconsiderate behavior. He promised he'd be home at a reasonable hour and—once again—he wasn't here.

I was on the couch watching a Lifetime movie when I heard his key clicking in the door. I could see him hanging up his cell phone, trying to hold his wallet and gym bag, while trying to close the front door. Unsurprisingly, just as the door slammed, everything fell to the floor.

I sprinted over to help him and noticed a few cards had fallen out of his wallet. I reached down and picked them up. Trying to organize them all in the same direction, one of them stood out from the rest.

"A hotel key to Harrah's in Atlantic City?" I questioned. "When did you go to Atlantic City?"

He hastily grabbed the cards from my hands and then told me

some story about how he had almost forgotten about it. It was from forever ago, when he went to his friend Shawn's bachelor party in New York City. I remembered the weekend he'd flown up there, but never remembered him mentioning a stop in Atlantic City.

"And you still have it in your wallet? Why would you save a hotel key?"

"Jesus Christ Haylie, what do you think, I'm lying to you? I guess I just thought I lost it and never turned it in."

"That's your story, is it?" I didn't want to tell him all the things I knew, but I was getting fed up with all his excuses.

"It's not a story, it's the truth, and I don't appreciate all your accusations."

"First of all, I didn't make any accusations Chase, and second of all, I was just pointing out the obvious."

"And what would that be Miss Know-It-All?"

"That you never mentioned any bachelor party taking place in Atlantic City, and that it is random to have a key to a hotel room hanging out in a wallet I bought you only six months ago." The color drained from his face as he searched for something to say. Once again, the only thing he could do was turn on his defense mechanism and make me look like the bad guy.

"You know, you're being a complete bitch right now, and I don't feel like dealing with it. I'm good to you, I take care of you, and this is what I get for it? I'm going to bed."

"Whatever," I spat, and watched him stomp up the stairs. I knew he hated that word, but at that point, I didn't care.

I peeked into the bedroom, about an hour after he'd gone

48

upstairs, to make sure he was asleep, and found him snoring. It was time I discovered some irrefutable proof, something he couldn't deny. I felt paranoid and guilty digging into his personal life, but not so guilty that I wouldn't do it. I felt like I was going insane. This woman I'd become, I didn't know her. Continuously stressed out, wondering at all times where my husband was, if I was making something out of nothing; it was becoming too much for me, but I knew. I knew something wasn't right. My gut was telling me the man I married was sharing his time and affections with someone else.

What was it going to take for me to be able to find the "Smoking Gun" I'd been looking for? No matter how much it might hurt, I needed to find the truth.

I crept downstairs into his office, sat behind his desk, and started to type. Whatever came to mind, I typed in. I'd known him for almost 10 years; I should've been able to figure out what his password was. I typed in my name, his first dog's name, the street he grew up on, our university mascot, and so much more; but no luck. "Password incorrect, try again" popped up over and over. After about twenty minutes, I could see goose bumps on my arms. My entire body was shaking in fear. Fear that any minute he was going to walk in and find me, fear that I was never going to find what I needed, but most of all, fear that I would.

"Think, Haylie," I whispered. I leaned back, looked up to the ceiling, and prayed. "God, I know I've asked you for a lot in life, and I know this probably isn't high on your priority list right now, but I need your help. I'm going crazy here. I don't eat, I can't sleep." Tears coursed down my cheeks and it was hard to say the words. "I just need some answers. I can't live like this anymore. I'm begging you, please help me." My final words slurred together as I succumbed to my sorrow.

What a mess I had become. I closed my eyes and tried to focus. This time I typed in the name of his law firm, his birth date, and our honeymoon spot. None of them worked. I kept trying. His mother's maiden name, the town she was born in; nothing. Then I got creative. I typed in his birth state of California backwards, San Diego backwards; still nothing. I had almost given up hope. I was running out of options. When I was about to stand up and call it a night, I looked up at the bookshelves that covered the wall across from the bay window, and there it was: his favorite movie of all time, The Sandlot. I typed it in and hit enter. This time, the entrance screen disappeared and his desktop popped up. I couldn't believe this is what my life had come to. Breaking into my husband's computer, not even knowing what I was looking for; but hoping that whatever it was, I would find it. I started clicking through folders, opening and closing documents, all while the voices of my friends echoed through my head. I could hear them telling me to just let it go, be happy with the life you have, turn your head, and just keep doing what you're doing. In a way, I did want to just brush it under the rug, because what I didn't know wouldn't hurt me; but in the end, I knew I couldn't live like that. It just wasn't in me. I was better than that, and I deserved better than that.

Most folders were just legal documents, client invoices, and case recaps. I actually began to feel relieved. It was just what I needed to find: nothing. If I couldn't find anything, it meant there wasn't anything there and I could finally put my accusations to rest and trust that my husband was telling the truth. My moment of joy, however, was short-lived when I clicked on a folder labeled Business Expenses. I opened a document labeled Charleston 5/10. It was a receipt for a condo rental. The date looked familiar, but I didn't know why. I got up, tiptoed into the kitchen, and looked at the planner on the fridge. On that weekend I wrote: Chase, Chicago until Sunday. I swallowed hard; my heart dropped. "That son of a bitch!" He never even went to Chicago. Tiptoeing back into Chase's office, I sat down again. The next file I opened was for a receipt for an airline ticket to Kettlewood Island for Labor Day. Cute, real cute! I wondered what his story would be for that weekend. I saved it to my email to print on a day while he was at work. If I was going to confront him, I was going to need this.

I searched a few other folders, but didn't find much, so I moved onto his email. My body was still shaking, and my mind and heart full of guilt. I had really become the crazy person Chase had accused me of being, but I couldn't help it. It was almost like I was looking at myself from the outside. Like I was watching some girl I didn't know, unable to control her actions.

There was nothing in his inbox. I thought maybe I'd find a receipt for an online flower purchase or an email from a woman to meet for dinner, but there was none. His sent folder, on the other hand, well that was a different story. At first I thought it was just spam. A bunch of "no subject" emails with an attachment being sent from him. I clicked on a random one dated three days ago. Nothing was written in the email, but there was a video attachment. I made sure the volume was turned down before I opened it. To my surprise, the still image of the video when it opened was Chase. Having no idea what to expect at that point, I hit the play button. At first Chase was just shuffling around, setting the camera in the right spot and moving the desk lamp around so he could be seen perfectly. I slowly turned the volume up just enough for me to be able to make out what he was saying.

"Hey baby, I'm about to go to bed and I just wanted to say goodnight. I miss you and I really hate sleeping without you, and knowing how long I have to go without seeing your pretty face is killing me. Labor Day is not going to come fast enough. Let me know when you're free this week for a phone chat. I don't want to go much longer without hearing that voice of yours. I will see you soon sweetheart."

The last thing I saw was him puckering his lips for the camera, sending a kiss across the airwaves. I clicked the X in the top right corner, signed out of his email, and turned off the computer as fast as I could. My face became flushed; I could feel it burning. I was so mad that I didn't know if I could keep from confronting him right then. My breathing became heavy, my fists clenched with anger. I wanted to scream, punch something, throw something, break something, and kick him where it hurt the most, literally. I wanted to run upstairs, shake him awake and ask him how he could ever do that me. I started to make my way up the stairs, imagining what I would say to him, but stopped just before I reached the room.

I could see it in my head. Flinging on the light, starting to scream at him; he'd call me crazy for going through his stuff and make up some lame excuse for the video I saw. He'd tell me I didn't know the whole story, that I took it out of context, or some other ridiculously stupid excuse he probably rehearsed in his head a thousand times. I certainly had everything I needed for my sake: I finally knew the truth. The question now was, what was I going to do with it? I had to gather my thoughts, put everything in perspective. I needed some time to gain courage. I wasn't ready to face him. So I turned around, went back downstairs and sat on the white porch swing. The stars obliviously twinkled in the clear North Carolina sky. I had just heard my husband confess his feelings to another woman. I was pretty sure my husband was sleeping with another woman. And worst of all; he looked me in the eye every day for months, lied to me, and never gave it a second thought.

I started to feel like a failure. Why wasn't I good enough? What did I do wrong? What could I have done differently? Then I felt nauseous. I was sickened by the thought that he would spend an entire weekend with someone else and then come home to me, make love, and hold me as I fell asleep. I forcefully rubbed at my arms; I felt so filthy. Dizziness seized me and I could feel the bottom falling out of my life. I stood up, leaned over the front porch, and vomited.

I sat back down on the bench, curled my legs in close to me, buried my head in my hands and cried. I cried for the end of my marriage, for the life I lived that was suddenly taken away. I cried for the now-unknown future. I thought about how I couldn't have seen it coming. How I was dumb enough to marry someone capable of this. How could I not have known? The signs, they had to have been there. I fought an exhausting battle with myself that night. Thinking of all the other times he'd gone away, all the other times his phone rang when he'd excuse himself from the room, and I wondered if it had all been her. Or maybe someone came before her. It was exhausting, running all of that through my mind. It didn't accomplish anything, and only made the tears fall harder.

It was almost three in the morning before I had stopped crying. I was so tired that I just couldn't cry anymore. My eyes were burning and I had a migraine. I knew I needed to go to sleep, but there was no way I could sleep in that bed tonight. I walked quietly inside and made a bed for myself on the couch. I'd simply tell him I fell asleep watching a movie. He probably wouldn't really pay much attention anyway; he never did anymore, and now I knew why.

Chapter 12

"Hey, sleepyhead, wake up." I could feel his hands shaking me from a deep sleep. I opened my eyes and looked up at him. He leaned over the couch, saying my name in that same innocent way he always did. He went on to apologize about our fight last night. Said he didn't mean to yell at me, but sometimes I just made him so angry that he didn't know what else to do.

Even having been up all night, I still had no idea what I was going to do. So until I figured it out, I had to pretend I was just an overreacting, jealous wife who was completely out of line.

"I'm sorry too, I don't know what got into me, it was just a long day and I took it out on you."

"Haylie, you know I love you, right? And you know I would never cheat on you? I don't know how you could ever think that."

Well, the video I found last night might have given me a clue. No, I didn't really say that out loud, but I wanted to. I just brought my hand up to my chest, wrapped my fingers around that heart-shaped necklace that I hadn't taken off since the day it was given to me, and smiled. "You certainly have given me more than I could have ever asked for, Chase."

"Well, I'm glad to hear that. I'm heading to the gym; I'll be back in a few hours and then maybe we could grab some lunch?"

I had no desire to be around him at all, but what choice did I have? "I don't think I'm really feeling up to lunch."

"Are you okay? You don't look well."

"Yeah, I'm fine; I think I'm just overtired. I'm going to lay here for a bit and rest."

"Okay, I'll be back to check on you later," he said as he kissed my forehead.

I used to feel so special when he did that. Now I just wanted to puke. As he walked out the door, my fingers released from the very first birthday present Chase had ever given me all those years ago. I felt the coldness of the silver as it rested back down upon my neck. I grabbed the pillow from behind my head, put it to my face, and screamed.

I just couldn't believe how someone could be so nonchalant about all of this. I mean, how heartless do you have to be to lie to the person you vowed to spend the rest of your life with? How can you wake up every morning and be fine with the person staring back at you in the mirror?

Ugh, I was so mad, I couldn't stand it. I had to figure out some way to get out of there, and fast. But I had nowhere to go. I didn't want my family to know what was going on. Not yet anyway; they would be devastated. I needed some time away to clear my head and figure out what I was going to do. He was my husband. I had invested seven years in this relationship, and I needed some time to think. I needed to do something other than sulk on the couch, cry, scream, and throw things. I'm sure everyone's first reactions are the same in a situation like this; but all I kept thinking was, what was it going to solve?

I'm glad I had an excuse to get out of having lunch with him. There's no way I was going to be able to handle that. He'd grab my hand from across the table, order for me like he always liked to do, and sweet talk me into forgetting any of this ever happened. I'd look at him the way a wife was supposed to look at her husband and I'd remember just how much I loved him. I'd leave there wanting to give him another chance. The problem was that he knew nothing so he would continue to do what he was doing, thinking he was getting away with it. He wasn't the Chase I married; he was a manipulative, egotistical liar who had done the worst possible thing anyone could do in a marriage.

I was working myself up so much just thinking about it, my stomach churned in knots. I felt sick again. I tried to ignore it, but it was impossible. I ran to the bathroom and threw up. I sat on the bathroom floor in a daze, Chase's voice echoing over and over again in my head: *I don't want to go much longer without hearing your voice. I will see you soon sweetheart.*

The tiles on the bathroom wall were cold against my back as I sat leaning against them, trying to be strong. *You'll be okay, Haylie; you'll be ok. People get through this all the time.* I pressed my head against the wall and cried. This time, I didn't try to hold it in. I know hind-sight is always twenty-twenty, and maybe five years from now I'd look back at this whole thing and know that it happened for some inexplicable reason and something good would come out of it, but at that moment, I felt like I was at a standstill. I couldn't move forward on my own, but the plans I had wanted to create with Chase had been destroyed. Life without him seemed unbearable, but I wasn't sure I could live it with him anymore, either. The hurt, the anger, the sadness, the overwhelming sense of guilt—no one ever deserves to feel like this. What made it even worse was that the pain was caused by the one person who promised never to hurt me.

All of this stress was taking its toll on me. I threw up two more times in the next hour. I didn't know how much more of it I was going to be able to handle. I couldn't go to lunch today; I couldn't go to lunch any day—not with him. I didn't want to see his face, I didn't want to hear his voice, and I certainly did not want him to touch me. I had to get out of there. Who knew where I would end up, but leaving was the only thing left to do.

The note I left on the kitchen counter didn't contain much detail. The only thing it said was, *I may be gone for a while. Let me be.* I wasn't sure what his reaction would be, nor did I much care. I thought about not leaving any note at all, but the last thing I needed was people scouring the neighborhood looking for me, expecting to find me lying lifeless in a ditch. I convinced myself I did it for them, for my friends; I didn't want them to worry. After calling work, (I told them I had a family emergency and would be taking a leave of absence) I threw my suitcase into the trunk of the Audi.

It was a relief there was no one around, as I didn't want to answer any questions. I just wanted to get out of there. I slid into the front seat, scrolling up and down through my phone contacts, hoping to come across someone I could call and talk to about all of this. Going through a situation like this, I knew my family would understand. I knew that all my close friends I still talked to from high school and college would completely understand my emotions and my choice to get away for a bit, but I still felt completely alone. I knew they wouldn't know how to comfort me, or what to say, and I didn't want them to see me for the mess that I was. I couldn't bring myself to call any of them. Throwing my phone on the passenger's seat and grabbing the steering wheel so hard my knuckles turned white, I knew where I had to go.

Chapter 13

Four hours later, and I was there. I drove along the main street area in the heart of Kettlewood Island. I wasn't sure where I was going to stay, but I knew this was where I needed to be. As much as I didn't want to think about it, didn't want to have to deal with it, I knew I had to face it. That's why I was here. I needed to re-evaluate my life, my marriage, who I was. I needed some time to just be alone and process it all, knowing that in just under two weeks, I would come face to face with it. She was going to be here then with *my* husband; in this quaint Carolina town. She, the woman who took my place, was going to be walking the beaches hand-in-hand with the man who pledged until death do us part: and I was going to confront them.

I pulled into a driveway with a weekly rental sign out front and walked inside. I was immersed in the sights and smells of the beach as soon as I opened the door. The pale blue walls were decorated with seashell and starfish pictures and beach-scented candles burned on the welcome table.

"How can I help you today?" An older woman, with wavy black hair, emerged from behind her desk.

"I'm looking to rent a beach house. I'd like to pay by the week, as I'm not sure how long I'll be here."

"You are lucky! We had a couple cancellations this weekend. I have a one-bedroom cottage about two miles from the beach, and a two bedroom beach-front cottage just around the corner."

I thought about waking up to the sound of the ocean. The peacefulness and serenity it would create. How great it would be to watch the sunset at night.

"I'll take the beach-front."

"Great! Have a seat and I'll get the paperwork."

After signing a few papers and handing over payment, I was walking up the stairs to my temporary home. The cottage was tiny, for a two-bedroom. A small, round table filled the dining area to the right of the entrance, and a small, rectangular living area was to my left. Mint green walls accented the floral print furniture. *Hmm, nice.* I walked past the kitchen into what appeared to be the master bedroom, as it had an attached bathroom. Outside the large window above the bed, I had a perfect view of the busy town. The sun may have begun to make its way toward the horizon, but this town was just waking up.

It had been a long day and I was exhausted, but I was surprised to realize I was hungry. It was time to see what food this town had to offer.

I hopped into the bathroom for a quick shower, dried my hair just enough so I didn't look like a drowned rat when I put it up, and added a little color to my pale demeanor with a smidge of eye shadow, mascara, and blush.

Before coming here, I frantically threw whatever I could grab into my suitcase, in fear I might change my mind. Now I wasn't sure what there was to choose from, outfit-wise. Throwing a few shirts aside and finally deciding on a simple blue maxi halter-dress, I slipped on a pair of black flip-flops and made my way onto the beach, in search of the nearest restaurant I could find.

I walked for about half a mile before something caught my eye. My flip-flops slapped my heels with each step, spraying sand up the backs of my legs. I passed charming jewelry stores and souvenir shops until I came upon the undeniable smell of fresh seafood. I followed the aroma, and loud Caribbean music, to an open-air seafood and steakhouse—The Pier Shack. I tried to ignore the fact that I was alone, but was soon reminded by the extra-bubbly hostess who greeted me at the entrance.

"Are you waiting for anyone this evening?" She gave a barely-there smile when I shook my head. After picking up one menu, she walked me over to a two-person table in the back. After quickly reading the specials of the day, she asked if I wanted anything to drink.

"I'll take a margarita on the rocks and a glass of ice water please."

"Sounds great. Meghan, your waitress, will be over shortly."

I opened my menu. I wasn't in the mood for steak, but all of their seafood options made my stomach groan even louder than before. My hunger made everything on the menu look delicious—I couldn't decide.

I was startled by the friendly welcome of my waitress. I had been so engrossed in the menu I hadn't seen her coming, drinks in hand. She was tall, way taller than me, not overly tan, but clearly it wasn't her natural skin tone, and her pin-straight black hair was pulled back into a low bun that showed off her hazel eyes. She was very pretty. I would have guessed she was around my age, but no one can ever be too sure these days. With pen in hand, she re-introduced herself and was ready and waiting for me to order.

"What do you recommend?" I asked.

"Tonight we have some great specials. The crab-stuffed flounder and ginger scallops are to die for. My favorite regular menu item is the Blackened Mahi Mahi over linguini in a cream sauce."

"They both are very enticing." I glanced over the menu one last time. "I think I'll try the crab-stuffed flounder."

Pasta seemed too heavy for my sick stomach and the scallops came with a side of potatoes I could do without. It's the one thing Chase always made fun of me for. Actually, I think it was the one thing everyone made fun of me for—my severe hatred of anything potatoes. Potato chips, French fries, you name it, if it was made with potato, I hated it!

I sipped water while waiting for my meal. I didn't want to have to deal with the consequences of downing tequila on an empty stomach. It wasn't long before my slightly over-tanned waitress came back with my dinner.

"Are you from the Kettlewood Island area?" I asked, hoping to unearth a good way to spend my time here.

"Born and raised," she laughed, and went on to tell me how growing up she couldn't wait to move to some big city like New York and land a corporate job. She had it all planned out, even a calendar counting down the days. "When it came down to it, though, I just couldn't leave the people I loved most. My whole family is here. Nine months of the year I teach high school English at the same school I graduated from. And summers I spend here, at The Pier Shack."

"Any particular reason why you chose The Pier Shack? I mean it's nice and all, but most teachers I know spend their time tutoring."

"My grandfather opened The Pier Shack almost 50 years ago. It's been in the family ever since. My dad took it over when I was in college." She paused and rolled her eyes. "He never hesitates to remind me that someday it'll all be mine."

"I take it you have a different plan?"

"I don't really have any plan, I guess. At the moment, I just go with the flow. I love being a teacher, and I am all about family, so most likely I'll end up doing what makes them happy. How about you? What brings you to Kettlewood Island?"

Caught off guard, I gave the vaguest answer I could think of and smiled. "I just needed a little *me* time."

"I hear you on that. It's always nice to get away every once in awhile and escape reality. I think that's why I always love being here in the summer. I can break free of the pressures of my friends getting married, having kids, and totally surpassing me on the 'what's expected' scale."

I nodded. I knew exactly how she felt. Everyone around me was having kids, and before this whole mess I was starting to get that itch too. I knew Chase and I were financially stable, and settled enough, to start a family. We had even talked about it a few times over the last year. Now all of that was out the window. I didn't know what the future held for the two of us, but I knew children weren't going to be the main focus of it anytime soon.

I extended my hand from the table and introduced myself. "I'm

Haylie, by the way."

For the first time since this whole thing started, I didn't feel so alone. We talked for a little while and Meghan gave me the tourist lowdown. She told me about the downtown area and its popularity for movie filming, and pointed out a few museums I might want to check out. An older couple sitting at a booth across the way called for her, and she bade me farewell as she rushed off to serve them.

When the food came, I ate like I hadn't eaten in weeks. My fork couldn't meet my mouth fast enough. I barely chewed each piece; almost choking a few times, stopping in between bites to sip on my margarita. The hunger I walked in with quickly changed to the need-to-unbutton-my-jeans feeling most people experience on Thanksgiving. I ate way more than I should've and was completely stuffed, but it was well worth it. I thanked Meghan for the helpful advice, gave her a generous tip for her southern hospitality, and headed to the beach for a walk.

The sun was just about to set over the water. I took off my flip-flops and walked along the edge of the sand where it met the waves of the ocean. It was funny; the entire drive to Kettlewood Island, I hadn't cried a single tear. I was angry, more than anything. Angry about how someone could throw their marriage away and hurt someone they claimed to love. During dinner, I was so focused on getting food in my stomach that it blocked out most of the pain; but now, now it was quiet. People were coming out of their hotels and beach houses for some nightly entertainment, but the noise was reduced to a murmur as the sound of the ocean drowned them out.

I didn't notice the chill of the water as it skimmed over my feet, as I was lost in the scenery. I stopped and watched as the sun met the ocean, and the sky burned with hues of red and orange. As the sun lowered into the ocean, and I breathed in the salty air, my vision blurred. My tears flowed freely, wetting my cheeks as the ocean had my feet. I hated myself for still loving him. After everything he'd done, how could I still love him? I stood there and stared, ingraining the image into my mind until the sun just about disappeared from the horizon. It left just enough light to guide me home.

That sunset confirmed that even though I couldn't see it now, all the hope in life was not gone. There was still beauty left in this world; even if I had to crawl, and be dragged on my knees for a while before I had the strength to stand, I would stand again. That is what I was here for. To find out who I was, what I wanted out of life, and what it would take for me to get there. I needed to understand what was happening to me, to my marriage, and whether or not it was worth fighting for.

I slipped out of my maxi dress and threw it onto the nightstand. I clipped my hair back and got ready for bed while wearing only the lace bra and underwear that was underneath. It had been my routine since I first moved in with Chase. I loved the way he looked at me when I was half naked. It made me feel sexy; wanted.

I traded my bra for my pink and black baby-doll chemise and grabbed my phone from the front pocket of my suitcase. I had three missed calls and two texts, from Chase. I ignored the voicemails, but read the texts. They sounded frantic, truly worried about where I had gone. If I hadn't known what he'd been up to the last few months I would've believed his concern, but I wasn't going to give in. If he really cared that I was gone, I wanted to let him sweat it out, show him what it's like to feel the angst I'd been feeling. I put the phone on silent, curled up under the comforter, and closed my eyes. Thanks to the margarita, I had no trouble falling sleep that night.

Chapter 14

I slept in later than I usually did. It was my body's way of telling me I needed to relax, and that is just what I had intended to do. With the temperature already in the mid 80s when I stepped out onto the balcony, it was the perfect day to lie on the beach. I closed my eyes and felt the sun upon my face. My hair blew off my shoulders and I could hear the faint sounds of seagulls, the ocean waves, and the squeals of children already out building their sandcastles. *It's going to be a good day,* I tried to convince myself.

When I dug into my suitcase for my bathing suit, I saw the blue light flashing on my phone. I was sure it was Chase, texting again, pleading for me to come home, or at least call him and tell him what was going on. Bathing suit in one hand, I grabbed my phone with the other and saw that it was Katie. *Chase came here looking for you. I didn't know what to say. Are you okay?* I texted her back with *Yes, I'm fine. Please don't worry.* I grabbed my beach bag and let the smell of hazelnut and mocha from the village coffee shop lure me outside.

The cute little coffee shop sat just up the street from my cottage. The smell of fresh-ground coffee is heavenly, first thing in the morning. As I perused the choices on the menu that hung the wall, I heard a familiar voice from behind.

"Making yourself at home, I see." It was Meghan, a far cry from her black-on-black waitressing ensemble last night. The navy blue one-piece suit, with side cutouts, was covered on the bottom by a sheer black wrap.

"I'm trying. Love your bathing suit. Your boss gave you the day off." I said, with a wink.

"Ha. The morning at least. Don't have to go in until four today. That leaves plenty of time to work on my tan. Much needed, as you can tell." She drew her hands from her head to her toes, showing off the obvious tan she already had. "Want to join me? I know the best spots on the beach. Unless you'd rather be alone?"

"No, that'd be great. Getting away was what I came here for, being alone just happened to come with the territory." I accepted her invitation, collected my frozen mocha, and we were on our way.

After lying there for a while in silence, Meghan gently tried to figure out what I was doing on Kettlewood Island. "I completely understand if you don't want to talk about it, but I do see you're wearing a wedding ring, and your husband is nowhere to be found. I'm a pretty good listener, so if you need an outsider's advice or just someone to vent to…" Her voice trailed off.

I was shocked at how easy it was to tell her about my situation. I couldn't bring myself to tell anyone close to me, but here I was, sharing intimate details about my life with a complete stranger. I'm not sure why, but I truly felt I could trust Meghan, and that she genuinely wanted to hear my story.

"I think my husband is having an affair. He doesn't know what I know yet. Before I tell him, I want to figure out what exactly I'm going to say and what I want to do about it."

"That's awful, I'm so sorry." She crinkled her nose. "I just don't understand men. You can't trust any of them. This is why I'm never getting married. Ring or no ring, they're all the same."

"I take it you're single?" I asked.

"I wouldn't consider myself in a relationship, but I've been seeing someone. It's been consistent for some time now, but my track record with men isn't pretty, so I'm playing it cautious; you know, taking things slow."

She told me they met at The Pier Shack. She had offered to show him around as he was new in town, and they'd been hanging out ever since. She went on to talk about how his job kept him on the road a lot, which she liked because it took the pressure off their relationship.

I didn't go into detail about what I had found to incriminate Chase, nor did I ever speak his name. I guess there just some things I wasn't ready to say. I told her how we had drifted apart, and he'd felt a lot of pressure trying to make partner, and how it'd been tough for me to fit into the neighborhood, as the women were all so different from me.

"Don't you do that," she blurted out. I looked at her. She could tell I was confused. "Don't you try to justify what he's done. This is on him, not you."

I smiled, if only at the simple fact that the last group of women, those who I considered my friends, suggested I brush it all under the rug and continue to live a lie. Here was this girl I barely knew, who knew nothing about me, my marriage, or where I came from, and she was standing up for me.

"You're only responsible for your own actions. You can hold yourself accountable for the mistakes YOU made, but you can't blame yourself for the choices HE made."

She had a point. I knew I wasn't perfect. I knew there were days even I didn't want to be around me, but you can bet just as much there were plenty of times Chase was not pleasant to be around either. I started, in my mind, to go off on a tangent. The anger built up again.

Marriage is not easy, I thought to myself. *It's not supposed to be easy. It's two different people, from two different backgrounds, trying to build a life together for better or worse. It's something you have to work at every single day. There are going to be hard times, and those are the times you are supposed to fight like hell. How hard are you willing to fight? The truth is, if you truly love someone, you'll use every ounce of energy you have until you have nothing left. That's what love is. The good times, those are the easy parts. Those are the parts of your relationship you get through the bad times for. You don't use the bad times as an excuse to jump into bed with some trashy whore who doesn't have enough respect for herself to say no to a married man!*

I stopped myself from going any further into thought, sighed, and rolled over onto my back. I refused to let him get the best of me. It was a gorgeous day and I was going to enjoy it. I had cried enough and felt enough hurt for years to come. I just wanted one day; one day of peace. I owed myself that much; he owed me that much. So I shut out all the happy families on the beach, and relaxed.

Chapter 15

Meghan and I lay on the beach for most of the morning and afternoon. It was nice having someone there. She didn't judge me, she didn't badger or lecture me; she just listened. And when I stopped talking, she'd lay back down and soak up as much sun as she could, before she had to leave to get ready for her shift at The Pier Shack.

By 2 p.m. it was time for Meghan to start packing up. I decided to follow her lead and call it a day as well. My stomach gurgled so ravenously as we were gathering our things that Meghan must have heard it too.

"You know where I think you should go?" she asked.

"Where?"

"The Sandbox Café. They have the best sandwiches in town."

I laughed. "It's that obvious, huh?" I said, looking down and patting my stomach.

"Just a little." She pressed her fingers together to gesture. "But for real, you should go. All their food is made fresh to order and the ingredients come from local farms."

"That sounds delicious. How far is it from here?"

"About ten minutes down that way. Just turn left when you see the sign for the East End Pier. I think it's the third traffic light. You can't miss it; it's a big green sign. The café is right on the pier, so you can sit outside and look at the ocean."

"Perfect. I'm gonna head home first to rinse off and freshen up."

"Let me know how you like it. I'll be at The Pier Shack all night, so stop by if you need anything."

"Will do. Thanks Meg."

We waved goodbye and headed in opposite directions.

Meghan was right—you couldn't miss the big green sign to the pier. As I made my way up the steps, I could see the line to the café was out the door and around the corner. She must not have been exaggerating about it being the best in town. I thought about all the other places I passed on the way, where I could go to get something to eat faster; but really, what kind of hurry was I in? Where did I need to be that I couldn't wait in line for a measly 15 minutes for a sandwich? The answer to that was nowhere. There was absolutely nowhere I needed to be. Today, this week, and maybe even the week after that, it was all about me. I was going to do what I wanted to do, as I figured out what the hell I was going to do with the mess I called my life. So, damn it: if I wanted to try the best sandwiches on Kettlewood Island, and I had wait 15 minutes to do it, then so be it—I would.

While waiting in line, I checked my cell phone. I hadn't looked at it since that morning and wondered if Katie had anything else to say about Chase showing up at her house. I could see the blue light flashing—a gentle reminder that life was still revolving outside the bubble I had retreated into.

There were four text messages and three voicemails. I saw that the only missed calls I had were from Chase. A lump grew slowly in my throat. My hands started to shake as I hit the delete button without even listening to the voicemails. I tried to do the same for his messages too, but I couldn't do it. I wanted to see what he had to say. I wondered if he knew why I left, was ready to confess what had been going on, or if he was going to continue to lie about it all. I guess I wasn't surprised that each one of them didn't allude to anything.

The first one read: *Can you at least tell me where you are? I need to know that you're okay.*

I clicked to the next one: *I love you, Haylie. Please come home and talk to me.*

And the next: *I'm going crazy here Haylie, please say something.*

"What's wrong?" I whispered, "What is bothering me, Chase is that you know EXACTLY what is wrong with me and you are too much of a coward to admit it!"

Mad, once again, at the ridiculous way he was handling this situation, I pounded the keys on my phone as I scrolled to the final text. It was Katie. *Glad you're okay. Call if you need anything. Be strong.* She was such a sweet girl. I remember the day she came over to bring us that apple pie. Her dark brown, shoulder-length hair was damp from the shower she must've taken right before. Her one-shoulder, navy blue Gucci dress hugged her figure perfectly. Her personality did not fit the image she tried to portray. She was sweet, bubbly, and level-headed. Just the kind of person I needed on my side at a time like this.

It took a lot longer than 15 minutes to reach the front of the line, but I found myself so engrossed in people-watching that the time went quickly. I watched a father hold an ice cream cone up to his little girl. She couldn't have been more than two. She fought real hard to try and hold it herself, but he stood his ground. Good thing he did, or he may have ended up like the poor mom who watched her son lick his chocolate yogurt right off his cone. He started crying before it hit the ground. She grabbed him and walked away before they became that afternoon's entertainment.

What really caught my eye was the young couple at a table just off the boardwalk. They couldn't take their eyes off one another. They held each other's hands from across the table. I smiled—thinking about how happy they seemed and remembering those days with Chase. How in love we were, how we wanted to spend every waking minute together. How we couldn't even get through a meal without wanting to put our hands on each other.

I wondered if it happened in every relationship. If the honeymoon phase really is just a phase. I wondered at this point how couples lasted fifty years. Maybe it was because my heart was broken and the pain was still raw, but it seemed to me that forever was really just a word in a song. All my friends back home existed in their marriages to keep their socialite status. Chase's parents divorced when he was young; and hell, every time I turn on E! another celebrity couple is heading for divorce.

My smile for that young couple faded. I wanted the happiness I saw in them. I wanted to be in love with someone who was truly in love with me. I wanted someone to want to come home to me after work, and miss me when I wasn't around. Could Chase and I get past this? Did I even want to try and work it out? Would he ever be able to tell me why? I just shook my head. By the time I looked up, it was my turn to order.

It was the biggest grilled chicken on flatbread I'd ever seen, and the taste didn't disappoint. It was just after four o'clock by the time I finished, and there was plenty of daylight left to explore. I knew a few hours of retail therapy wasn't going to fix all that had been broken, but it seemed a good place to start. I needed some time to step away from my thoughts and regroup, hoping I would be able to come back to them later and delve into every angle of the situation. I had cried enough the last few months—shopping followed by a scenic stroll on the boardwalk might do me some good.

It was late evening by the time I returned to my cottage, but like many nights before, I wasn't ready to go to sleep. I grabbed a wine glass from the cupboard and poured myself some of the Moscato I had picked up on my way home. Since the sun had gone down long ago, I sat on one of the Adirondack chairs on the back deck and watched the waves ascend upon the shore, creating a ripple effect each time they disappeared back into the ocean. The moonlight glistened off the water, and distant shadows sauntered at the far end of the beach.

I sat there for a long time, just thinking. The gentle hissing as the waves made their way up to shore was the only sound that echoed. You would have thought I'd get sick of thinking about the same things over and over again, but I couldn't help it. I re-played every scenario in my head. Where they met, what she looked like, could I have prevented this? There was just so much to worry about, to wonder about. Did he love her? That would have broken my heart the most. I might have been able to deal with an infatuation, lust, inner struggles to find himself: but not love. I don't think I could've handled it if he really had fallen in love with her.

Two heavy eyes and an empty bottle of wine later, it was time to call it a night. I wiped the tears that had unknowingly fallen upon my face, took one last look at the moonlit sky, and headed inside. It was the first night I could remember that I actually slept soundly. Thankful for the miracle a bottle of wine could bestow, I was free from my thoughts until the morning.

Chapter 16

The next morning, I had trouble getting out of bed. My head was spinning, and when I lifted it from the pillow it seemed to weigh a hundred pounds. I was never a fan of the consequences of a night of drinking, and it was even more pathetic that it was a night of drinking alone. As I'd learned from the few nights in college that I had partied too hard, the best cure for me was to sweat it out. After procrastinating for a half hour, I dragged myself out of bed, dressed in my running gear, and hit the beach.

It was the most painful workout I had endured in a long time. Not because I had worked myself past my comfort zone, but because it took everything I had not to stop and throw up. I kept telling myself it'd be better once all the toxins were sweated out of me, so I continued to run. I was far into my run, and was about to turn around, when I saw Meghan waving at me from what must have been her beach bungalow. I jogged up to her, hoping she wouldn't notice the fragile state I was in, but no such luck.

"You look like shit."

"Ha! Gee, thanks."

"A little too much partying last night?"

"You know it. Me, a big blue chair on the deck, and a bottle of wine."

"Pity party for one, huh?"

I nodded. She placed her hand on my shoulder, and then disappeared inside for a minute. She returned with a bottle of water and handed it to me. After guzzling almost the entire bottle in one gulp, I sat down on the wood bench on her deck; she leaned against the railing, staring out towards the water.

"I've been there, you know."

"Been where?"

"Where you are right now. I mean, I was never married, never had a ring on my finger, but I was expecting one at any minute."

"Do tell."

"I started dating this guy, Rick, in high school. Four years after graduation, we were still together. I thought he was the one. My family did too. Everyone talked about us getting married all the time. The two of us included. Just a few months before we finished college, we were talking about the best time of year for a wedding. He even took me to look for engagement rings. Told me he didn't want to put something on my finger for the rest of my life without me having some sort of say in it." Her eyes looked to the ground.

"Sounds like it was pretty serious."

"Leading up to Christmas of that year, that's all my mom could talk about. She even took me to the nail salon a few days before Christmas Eve, just to make sure my nails were prepped and ready to show off the ring." We both laughed at how crazy that sounded. "Christmas came and went, and still no ring. He cancelled our plans for New Year's, and a few days later asked me to meet him in town. He ended it right then and there with no explanation at all. He kissed my forehead as I cried in the street, got in his car, and drove away."

I could feel the tears welling in my eyes. "That is the saddest thing I've ever heard. Did you ever hear from him after that?"

"Not a word. I cried for days, wondering what it was I did wrong. A few weeks later, I saw him walking out of a restaurant on the other side of town, hand in hand with another girl. They looked like they knew each other pretty well."

"What a jerk. Seriously." I placed my hand upon hers and tried to blink back my unshed tears.

"That's not even the last of it. A few months after I saw him with that girl, he called me and asked to meet for dinner. Trying to stay strong, I told him I already had plans. That excuse only worked for so long, though. Eventually I gave in. He begged for me to take him back and told me how big of a mistake he had made."

Unfortunately for Rick, his groveling had no effect on Meghan and the status of their relationship stayed the same. She was adamant about not giving second chances, as she fully believed in the saying, "Fool me once, shame on you; fool me twice, shame on me." Meghan, though not knowing her for too long, seemed like someone who refused to be played for a fool.

"I didn't cry again until he walked out of the restaurant. It took many more nights of crying in my pillow, and watching Friday night TV with a pint of ice cream in my lap, before I was able to put it all behind me; but eventually I did."

At least that's the story Meghan told me. It may have been just me, but I swear I saw a glimmer of pain pass through her eyes at the very moment she said that. I think we all learn to move on from the pain in our lives, but it doesn't mean the scars don't still exist. During moments like this, the drudging up of the past, the hurt is still very much there. Not wanting to think about it any longer, Meghan gently pounded her hand on the deck railing and turned to me.

"And you're going to move on, too! And you'll be a much better person because of it."

"Thank you, I needed that," I said. Until I did move on, though, Meghan was not going to let me drown my sorrows in some cheap bottle of wine.

"Now run back home, literally, and get ready for a girls' day. Today is my day off, and you and I are going to have some fun. I'll pick you up at eleven, so be ready. Go; get running."

"Alright, I'm going. I'll see you in a couple of hours."

I gave her the address to my beach cottage and was on my way. I was very impressed that I had run four miles and almost, yes almost, made it home without getting sick. With only about a quarter mile to go, the night before finally caught up with me. My face met the nearest garbage can it could find, and made its acquaintance for a few minutes. The rest of the way home was a slow and steady walk.

After a cold shower, I felt a million times better and got ready for another gorgeous day. Meghan's story gave me a little bit of hope. She seemed happy with her life, and even had a new man, which meant she had actually opened herself up to the possibility of loving again. It was a good thing I had met her. She reminded me very much of my best friend from back home in Rochester. Her name was Lauren. She had the same long, black hair as Meghan, but wasn't nearly as tall.

Lauren was one of those people who, no matter how bad things were in your life, she always knew how to find the good in it. She'd give you hope when you thought there was none. She was one of those rare people in your life that you could always count on. Even with her busy life, raising two kids under the age of five, she always made sure she took the time to call me each and every week to check in. I felt like Meghan was that kind of friend for me at the moment. When I first got to Kettlewood Island, I thought I needed to be alone. I wanted to spend all my time locked away in my room, crying, sulking, and being angry. I slowly realized that feeling sorry for myself wasn't going to do me any good.

As Chase's wife, I'd done things I thought would make him happy to the point that I lost myself along the way. I prepared dinner every night like a wife was supposed to do. I got dressed up in fancy dresses and walked arm in arm with him to every work holiday party. I paid all the bills, kept the house in order, and made a fresh appetizer every Saturday for the neighborhood brunch get-together.

I couldn't remember the last time I just sat down to read a book, or watched a movie at the theater—did something just for me. Now don't get me wrong, before all of this, I loved being Chase's wife. It was just that, early on in our relationship, I was able to balance Chase time with *me* time. It seemed like I hadn't done that in awhile. Instead, I did what was expected of me. After reminiscing on how my life had turned out, I was ready to go out and have some fun.

Meghan pulled up in her Volkswagen convertible. I hopped in and we drove along the coastline, just admiring the scenery.

"Where are you are taking me?" I asked.

"You're very lucky you're hanging with a local. You'll learn all the secret hot spots in no time," she joked.

"Are we are heading to one of those hot spots?"

"Yes ma'am. There is this amazing homemade popsicle shop just north of Kettlewood Island. You are going to love it."

"You're telling me we've been driving all this time for a popsicle?"

"Like you had anything better to do. And yes, a popsicle that's to-die-for."

I think Meghan's mouth was already watering by the time we pulled up to a cute little store-front. "Mango-infused watermelon is my absolute favorite." She literally skipped to the front door. Looking at the menu above the register, she let me know her opinion of each and every flavor. It was clear she went there often.

"I'm going to go simple for my first time. Can't get too crazy, you know. I'd like the pineapple and coconut please."

The girl behind the counter handed me the popsicle and, after one taste, I had to admit Meghan was right: it was well worth the drive. On top of the peaceful, scenic drive up here, the popsicle was delicious.

In between licks of her fruity creation, Meghan would quickly text on her phone, making sure to hit send each time before she lost any drips. We stood outside in silence for a while. She was distracted. I could tell by the smile on her face it must have been the 'sort of' boyfriend she had mentioned before. I teased her about her expression, and she laughed.

"He says he has something important to talk to me about, but wants to do it face to face. I'm not sure if I should be worried or not."

"Any idea what you think it could be?" I asked.

"Not even the slightest. He'll be back next week. Said I have to wait until then."

"I'm sure it's a good something. No need to be worried. You guys are good, right?"

"Never better," she assured me.

I nudged her side in shared excitement and she jokingly pushed me away as if to say, *you're so fresh.*

"So, are you happy we came?" Meghan asked.

"I am."

"Finish that up. We have some shopping to do. We need to find you some single-girl clothes."

I was uneasy at that comment. Still torn by what I was actually going to do, Meghan's words made it all seem so final. To me, final was still the furthest thing from my mind. Not wanting to seem ungrateful for all she'd been doing for me, I just smiled and went along for the ride. We did some shopping at the boutique stores that surrounded the popsicle shop, and then headed back to Kettlewood Island for dinner. To no surprise, the last place Meghan wanted to go for dinner was her family restaurant. She loved working there, and of course the food, but it was nice to change it up. We went to a local burger place a few miles from the beach. Meghan ordered a cheeseburger, and I settled on a grilled chicken salad with a side of honey mustard.

We sat there for a few hours and talked. We talked about what made her decide to become a teacher, her family, and my crazy housewives back in Charlotte. One thing we didn't talk about, though, was Chase. Meghan made sure to skip that subject completely. She was determined not to let him get to me. She kept telling me how strong I was, how I would do great things in life, and how I was still young and had so much more life to live. I wanted to believe her. I wanted to believe I was a strong person—that I could hold it together when things fell apart, and that I could stand up to Chase and hold my ground. But that night proved her wrong. It proved me wrong. What a mess it was.

I planned on going to bed early. The sun had just set and I was already home, comfy in my pajamas. I hadn't heard from Chase all day, but that changed once I was in bed with the TV on. When I first saw his name light up on my cell phone screen, I jumped. I tried hard to ignore it at first and just let it ring. After the first four or five continuous calls, ignoring it became a challenge. My phone beeped with voicemail after voicemail and didn't stop. It continued for an hour before I couldn't take it anymore. I fought with everything I had until finally, I grabbed the phone from my nightstand and answered it.

At first it was silent. I didn't even say hello, but my breathing was so heavy I knew he could hear me. My name, in a quiet whisper, came through the phone. I let out a deep sigh and closed my eyes for a long minute. I held on to that quiet whisper. It was the way he would always say my name in bed when he couldn't sleep and wondered if I was still awake.

"Haylie, please talk to me?" I wanted to talk to him. I had plenty of things to say. Good things, bad things, mean things, there was so much I wanted to say, but nothing would come out.

"Come home, Haylie." Finally, with my eyes still closed, I spoke to him.

"I'm not coming home, Chase. Not yet, I need a little time away to figure things out."

"I don't understand what you are trying to figure out. I didn't do anything wrong, Haylie. I don't know why you think that."

My body clenched up. The calmness and comfort from hearing him say my name immediately disappeared. I was angry once again. He was lying to me, and I knew it. I wanted so badly to tell him that I saw his video. That I knew about his secret vacation plans, but I couldn't bring myself to. Maybe it was because then he would know there was no way out, and I would actually have to hear the words come out of his mouth. I would know the truth, and there would be no escaping it. Or maybe it's because he would've told me I was crazy—that I was making something out of nothing and I would start to believe him. I wanted to be as strong as Meghan thought I was, but I couldn't, at least not at that moment. It was too raw. I said nothing.

"I love you, Haylie. I would never do anything to hurt you. You know that. Seriously, just to even know you could ever think I'm capable of something like this—it kills me. Please come back, babe. Lets talk about this."

I was amazed at the real sound of sincerity in his voice. Like he actually believed what he was saying. If there was one thing I knew for sure, one thing that had come into fruition these last few days, it was that somewhere along the path of our relationship, Chase had become a very good liar.

"I need more time," I finally said. "This is all just too much to handle right now. I just want to be alone."

"How much time?"

"I don't know. Another week or two."

"So you won't be home for the long weekend?"

"No," I said. "Please Chase, just leave me be for now. When I'm ready to talk, I'll let you know. Until then, I just need to be left alone."

"I hate this. I just want to hold you and show you how much I love you."

"I am asking you to do this one thing for me."

"Okay, I will give you space. I love you, Haylie. Remember that."

It was hard to hear those words. I didn't respond. There was nothing I could say to that. I hung up the phone and cried myself to sleep.

Chapter 17

Chase had listened to my request and he stopped calling me. I know he had done what I asked him to, but I still wondered if it bothered him—if it took great strength for him to not pick up the phone, or if he was too preoccupied with work…or her. Perhaps, since he knew I wasn't going to be home anytime soon, he'd call to meet up with her. Or maybe he spent his nights waiting for her call instead of mine.

I'd cried often since that night. I thought about how Chase and I met, and how happy we were on our wedding day, and all we'd been through as a couple. It was heartbreaking to end it and scary to even think about trying to find that same passion with someone else. How does someone who's given their entire heart to someone, and loved someone with all they have, ever let someone else in so intimately again? I struggled with the fact that I wasn't good enough. That someone else had given my husband what I couldn't. No feeling in the world was worse than that.

Finding out your husband is having an affair is pretty similar to the grieving process one goes through when losing a loved one. You grieve for what you've lost, try and remember the good times you had with them and then, at some point, you learn how to find peace in a memory. I hadn't gotten that far yet. I was still grieving—for what I had not put an end to yet, and for what I knew I had to come face to face with.

The next few days went just as quickly as the last. I continued my morning workouts and sometimes Meghan joined me. During the day, the two of us went to local boutiques for shopping, toured a few of the local museums and, of course, made sure we spent some time lounging on the beach to get a tan. There were times here and there when I would see Meghan check her phone, smile, and text back.

I could tell she was excited for her reunion with the guy sending those texts. She never said much about it; I think it's because she wasn't ready to accept that she'd really fallen for him. She wanted to play the tough girl. She liked to show the strong, independent, don't-need-anyone-to-take-care-of-me attitude. But I could see it by the way she jumped off her towel each time to grab the phone. Her silent laughter at whatever conversation they were having made it obvious she was invested. Good for her, I thought. She had become the person I believed I needed to be. Sure, I thought about going home, talking to Chase and putting it all behind us. Maybe if he was truly sorry for all he had done, we could move past it and rebuild the life we had planned. However, as much as I'd hoped, I didn't see it as a real possibility. There was too much he had hidden from me and lied about; my trust in him had disappeared. I knew in my heart that there was no excuse for what he was doing. If he was unhappy in this relationship, if he was having trouble connecting with me, then he should have come to me about it. He should have let me in on what he was going through. Instead, he gave up. He took the easy way out and, like Meghan said, this was his choice. A choice that he made willingly. This was not an it-just-happened-in-the-heat-of-the-moment mistake. There was no way out of it. I knew deep down what was broken could not be fixed. I would have to start over.

I had to learn to depend on myself now. It was time to take care of myself, and focus on what I wanted. The hardest part was already done. I had walked out, made the first move to leave, even if it was just for a little bit. I was sending a message to Chase that this type of behavior was unacceptable, and that I wouldn't stand for it. It was just one step, the first of many, but don't they always say: the journey of a thousand miles begins with one step.

I had just a few more days left on Kettlewood Island, as Labor Day was quickly approaching. The last week and a half had gone by way too quickly. For one of our last dinners together, Meghan relented and we went to The Pier Shack. It was the lobster tail and crab leg special that hooked us. I was keen on crab legs. I could eat an entire plate in one sitting and probably still want more. It was in between shell cracking and tail peeling that I tried to pry into Meghan's love life. I started off asking when she was expecting his arrival.

"He said it will definitely be sometime before Labor Day." She didn't talk much about what he did, just said he owned a bunch of stores on the east coast and regularly had to travel to them to make sure they were running smoothly.

"You have to meet him. The three of us will go to dinner one night."

"I thought three was a crowd?" I joked.

"No way! Not at all. I want you to meet him. It would really mean a lot to me. I feel like you and I have been friends for years. Our friendship is important to me."

"Well, if you put it that way." I said. I pulled my phone out of my pocket and pretended to check my calendar. "It looks like I'm pretty wide open the next week, so you're good."

She threw her head back, laughing. "So glad you can squeeze me in."

Chapter 18

Over the next couple of days, Meghan was busy with both of her jobs. She was trying to keep up her shifts at the family restaurant, while covering for the kids who left to go back to college, on top of preparing her classroom and welcoming back students for the new school year. As busy as she was, she always made the time to come over on her way home to check up on me and make sure I wasn't drowning in a bottle of wine or crying my mascara off. I laughed at the thought of it, even though sometimes I actually was. I did my best to take my mind off things—maybe more for her sake than my own. Poor Meghan wanted so badly to show me there was life beyond my pain, and I wanted her to believe she was helping me figure that out.

I couldn't sleep the Thursday before the Labor Day weekend began, knowing that tomorrow, if Chase was bold enough, he would be getting on a plane and heading this way. Was he packing for his romantic rendezvous? Or was he making the phone call to cancel his plans, telling her he couldn't see her anymore? Was his wife, and the life they had together, more important to him than his relationship with someone he barely knew? Tomorrow, we would find out. I knew his plane landed at 2 p.m. from the receipt on his computer, but I had no idea where he'd go from there. I wasn't planning on searching for him,

I just sort of hoped fate would lead me in the right direction. I just had to wait, be patient, and hope I could finally get some answers.

Knowing that Meghan would probably be knocking on the door at a late hour when her shift was done, I stayed up on the couch flipping through a few magazines that were left by the prior tenant. It was just before eleven when she came running up the deck. I'd wondered what she was so excited about. She flung open the sliding glass door and had a big grin on her face.

"I'm sorry; I'm going to have to cut our visit a little short tonight."

"Everything okay?"

"Couldn't be better. He's here." She bounced about in happiness. Her smile was beaming.

"Look at you, like a kid in a candy store."

It seemed her special someone was finally home from his business travels. He'd surprised her at work, and I'm sure she hadn't stopped smiling since. I was happy for her. She was overjoyed and quite different from the reserved woman I'd spent all this time with. I shared in her excitement until she had to go.

"Don't think you're off the hook. Just because I have company, doesn't mean you can go back to sulking. "

"I wouldn't dream of it. If I'm not here, I'll probably be getting my tan on. I have a lot of hours left before I catch up to you."

"I will, however, have to leave you on your own for tomorrow morning's run. I'm not planning on getting much sleep tonight."

"Um….way too much information," I laughed as she pranced down the stairs to the beach.

I watched as she got into her car. I could see a dark figure in the passenger seat as she pulled away. So he was finally here. The man that obviously had a reverse effect on the head-strong woman I'd gotten to know so well. It was hard to be happy for someone else when you were so miserable, but this was a big step in Meghan's life, as we'd talked about a few nights before.

I was getting used to the distraction Meghan created with her nightly visits. Sitting alone only caused my mind to wander in the direction of Chase. That night wasn't any different. Without Meghan, it was impossible to think of anything else, but I tried. I read every magazine on the coffee table from cover to cover. When I would find my mind start to drift into a sad memory, I'd quickly pull myself out of it and get back to reading.

An hour or so had passed, by the time I had finished. My eyes were heavy at that point, my body begging me for rest. Picking myself up off the couch, I headed into the bedroom to cozy myself up underneath the covers. It took few deep breaths in and out before the room turned to a fog, but within minutes my mind finally gave in and I was able to escape the reality that stood before me.

Chapter 19

The weather was perfect for running on that Friday morning. Slightly overcast with a cool breeze. I dug into my suitcase to find some workout clothes, tightened up my laces, and headed out the door. I put in my earphones and hummed along to the music as my feet steady paced through the sand.

The sun was getting hot about a mile in, sweat pouring from every part of me. I thought about turning around and cutting my distance in half, but it's never been in me to give up that easily; so I kept running. Running away the minutes of the morning, the sorrows of yesterday, and right into the crumbling of my entire world.

It was thanks to my handy iPhone app, which told me it was exactly two miles from my beach house to Meghan's. I could see it coming up as I slowly pushed up the slight hill. My eyes were blurry from the sweat and the heat, but through them I could see someone emerge from Meghan's beach house: someone that was clearly not Meghan. I was too far away to see any clear features, but I could tell it was a man. He was quite tall, wearing no shirt, and his hair was maybe a sandy brown. His face was turned away from me, but I could see his arm rise up as he lifted his hand to his mouth to sip on what I figured was a cup of coffee.

As I ran closer, his silhouette came into focus—I could see the outline of his chin, his broad shoulders, muscular chest, and yes, it was sandy brown hair. It was a little disheveled, as he'd obviously just woken up. From what I could see, I had to applaud Meghan on her choice of men. He was tall, athletic, and only his bottom half was clothed. He was nice to look at with no shirt on.

Maybe it was the fact that I had been alone for so long, but for some reason I just couldn't take my eyes off the stranger. I kept my eyes fixated on him as he turned his head towards me. You know those times in movies when that triumphant, romantic music is playing while a boy and a girl are running towards each other, and then it suddenly gets interrupted by one of them falling flat on their face? Well, this was one of those moments. He was looking in my direction and there was no mistaking it. It took a minute for it to sink in. It was the last thing in the world I expected to see, but there it was. Impossible to miss. The vision I'd seen a million times before. Even from this far away, it stood out clearly.

I stopped running. Sweat dripped into my open mouth. I couldn't stop staring. I followed the lines of his body from head to toe, and back up again. Engraving each part into my brain just as if I was studying for a biology test. Making sure not to leave any of it out. I wanted to be sure, more than sure. And I was.

He hadn't noticed me yet: he was too distracted by the waves of the ocean and the coffee in his hands to see me coming his way. But I'd know those eyes anywhere. They'd looked at me countless times in the last several years. Including the day they stared into mine and vowed to love me, honor me, and always be faithful until death do us part.

I blinked, several times, but it didn't matter, nothing was going to change. Like a boulder, barreling down a mountain towards me, there was no time to move, no escape plan, nothing to be done, but close my eyes and brace myself. The worst possible scenario was happening. The man Meghan told me to forget about, the man she told me I was stronger than, and the man she was hopeful was going to take the next step with her in their relationship, they were one in the same. The man that stood on Meghan's deck at that very moment was Chase. Meghan was in love with my husband.

"How could I not have known?" I said out loud to myself. I'd wondered how I hadn't picked up on something like this. The entire time we talked, she was talking about my husband; I was talking about her boyfriend, and neither of us figured it out. Thinking back on it, neither of us ever said his name or described his features. And the man Meghan talked about, the business-man, he didn't even exist. He was not a real person. The man that woke up in Meghan's bed this morning was a high-powered lawyer from a small town outside of Charlotte, North Carolina. He'd been married for five years, and he and his wife bought a traditional Southern-style house with a wrap-around porch on a cul-de-sac street where they planned to raise their children, get a dog, and be the typical, happy Southern family they'd always talked about.

Now, that was all gone—taken from me. I'd known there was someone else for quite some time, and I thought that when Chase admitted it, or I found him walking the streets of Kettlewood Island hand-in-hand with another woman, it would merely confirm what I already knew. I thought I could handle it, that it wouldn't break me down like it was. And what made it even worse was that the girl I had come to trust, the girl I had poured my heart and soul out to, cried to and leaned on during all of this, was the same woman. She was the girl on the phone in the car when he'd arrive home from work at night. She was the girl who received the video message I'd seen on Chase's computer, and the text message. Oh God, this is what she was talking about. This was the moment she was counting down the days for. I kicked myself for never exchanging numbers with her. If I had, I would have known right then and there. That number was burned into my memory from those phone records; I would've recognized it immediately. If only I hadn't lived right down the beach, then maybe there would have been an actual need for it. The girl who ruined my life, the reason I cried myself to sleep at night for the past few months, was Meghan.

I became irrational, standing on the beach by myself. So many thoughts were flying through my head. I bet she knew this whole entire time. No way, now that I know, could it have been a coincidence. She befriended me on purpose. She wanted to see what kind of a person I was, so she could justify her affair with MY husband. *That two timing little bitch.* I'd had enough of these games. Enough of the lying. That was it: I was done.

My legs finally came to life and I started moving. I walked quickly—closer and closer to Chase. Still oblivious that someone was on the beach below him, I walked right up to the bottom of the stairs. I glared at him, rested my forearm on the railing and set my right foot on the first stair. It took a minute for him to notice me, and maybe even another for him to recognize who I was. He looked at me. I glared back. Nobody moved, and nobody said a word. His lips twitched a couple of times, but still he didn't speak. He knew. He knew nothing he was going to say was going to get him out of this. Nothing he could say would be the truth, and nothing he was going to say I would believe. He remained silent.

My mind reeled with everything that I had wanted to say to him. *How could you, did you think I wouldn't find out, I hate you* and so much more, but I was so angry that I couldn't say any of it. I was so concentrated on him, and the fact that he was standing on my friend's porch half naked, that I barely heard the sliding glass door open as Meghan walked out.

"Haylie!" She seemed so excited to see me.

I just wanted to spit nails at her, punch her in her pretty little face, and maybe even throw her down these stairs. She was lucky that those stairs separated us, because I wasn't sure what I was capable of. It's like they say, hell hath no fury like a woman scorned.

I wondered why, with so much to say, that I couldn't scream and yell at Chase. I could glare at him, I could be angry at him, but I couldn't say a damn thing to him. To Meghan, however, there was plenty I had to say, and I said it.

My voice came across like daggers. "How could you? Every single day for the last two weeks I confided in you. I trusted you. You saw how much pain I was in; you saw me cry." My words were shredded by my anger, almost incoherent. I didn't realize I had begun to cry. The tears drowned out the words as they hit my lips. I went on and on, screaming every profanity that I could think of to belittle her and put her down. I would have kept going, too, if she didn't interrupt me.

"Haylie, what the hell is going on with you?" I looked at her, then at him, and back at her again. She looked at Chase with wondering eyes and then, from the look on his face, she realized what was going on. She turned pale, the life drained right out of her. She fell to the seat below and placed her hand over her mouth. She didn't know. She really didn't know. She was just as blindsided by this as I was. I wanted to feel sorry for her, but I couldn't, at least not right then. Anyone else would want to hug her, console her just as she did me, but I couldn't. My hatred was too strong.

I understood it now. The guys-only trip Greg and Chase went on some time ago—they'd both agreed upon Kettlewood Island. It was the same distance for both of them; Greg was driving down from Richmond and they had a strong desire to try fishing somewhere new. It made sense now that he would come back here on Labor Day, but the rest of Meghan's story—none of that seemed to add up. The traveling salesman. It sounded like a story out of a book. I just didn't understand any of that.

Chase stood there, one hand on the railing still holding his coffee cup, the other hung by his side. His body faced Meghan, and he was staring at the ground. I pushed myself away from the stairs, shook my head, and continued to cry.

As I backed away, Chase came down the stairs towards me.

"Haylie, please." He reached out for me, but I refused to let him get any closer. I screamed at him to stay away. I told him to go to hell. The faster he came down those stairs, the faster I moved away.

"Don't you dare!" My words were loud and forceful. "Don't

you dare try to make this better, because you can't."

"Will you just calm down for one second?"

"Calm down? Calm down? No, I will not calm down. I hate you. I hate you so much." I said it a few more times, even though it was a lie. I wasn't crying because I hated him. I wasn't angry because I hated him. I loved him. I loved him with everything that I was, and everything that I had. That's why I was angry. I couldn't control myself at that point, so I ran. I ran as fast as I could towards home. I could hear myself gasping for air as the wind brushed my tears across my cheeks.

I could see people staring at me, whispering, wondering what this crazy woman was doing, but I didn't care. I just kept running, sobbing. It was all I could do. The closer I got to my house, the fewer people were around. Finally, when nobody was in sight, I couldn't hold myself up anymore. I collapsed to my knees, violently shaking until I finally fell into the fetal position. I lay there with my knees curled to my chest, letting my tears sink into the sand.

There I stayed, for a very long time. My body was physically in pain, as well as my heart. The lowest moment in my life had finally come. There I was: 28 years old, crying alone on the beach. I had nobody. There was nothing that was going to make this better. Not only had my husband cheated on me, but I had spent the last two weeks watching the woman he'd cheated with texting him, yearning for him, and smiling about him. And for God's sake, less than 24 hours ago she had jokingly told me how she knew she wouldn't be getting much sleep that night. That image sucked the last of my strength from me as I lay there. I tried to get it out, but I couldn't. He had made love to her, held her close to him all night long, while I was just two miles down the beach. While I was preparing for a typical morning run, he was waking up beside her. Was it possible for someone to be so cruel and cold-hearted? I just could not understand how anyone could ever do this to someone they loved.

I wouldn't wish this sort of agony on my worst enemy. It was pure and complete torture. To know that, for the man who made up my entire world, I was not enough for him. There was no feeling I had ever felt that was worse than that. If ever such a feeling did exist, I prayed to God that my life's journey would never bring me to it.

Chapter 20

After an hour of crying, I finally gained the strength to pick myself up off the now tear-stained beach long enough to make it back home. I closed the sliding glass door behind me and made sure to lock it. I didn't know if either of them would, but if they did come over here, I sure as hell did not want them in my house.

I stripped off my sweaty, sand-filled clothes and turned on the shower. As I waited for the water to warm up, I glimpsed myself in the full-length mirror. I turned towards it and really stared at myself. There I was, as vulnerable and as naked as I was the first time Chase and I had made love. I pressed my hands against my stomach and wondered if maybe this wasn't attractive to him anymore. Maybe I wasn't as pretty as I was back then. Maybe I wasn't as skinny. There had to be something. Something about me that made him do this. I grabbed the towel that rested on the sink and hurled it at the mirror. I was disgusted with myself. I stepped into the shower and let the water drown my tears.

With my eyes closed, it was all so vivid. There I was, on my daddy's arm, walking down the aisle to the man of my dreams. The day we signed our closing papers with the bank and took home the keys to our very first home. Chase pulling in the driveway with the Audi he bought me for my 26th birthday—a total surprise I never saw coming. I saw his bright smile greeting me in bed in the morning, and felt his soft lips kiss me goodnight. How happy we used to be.

Those images were all washed away by that same smile I saw as he hung up the phone in his car, parked in the driveway after work. In my head, I saw him get out and walk up to the porch of our perfect little home and open the front door. He closed it behind him and put his arms out for a hug. There she was, waiting for him in my house, wrapping her arms around my husband. Her long black hair pressed by his hand against her back. She had taken over my dreams: in my head and in reality.

I stepped out of the stream of water and opened my eyes. That sweet, tall, almost overly-tan waitress would forever taint my thoughts. She had been my most trusted companion during these last couple of weeks, introducing me to mouth-watering popsicles, boutique shopping, and lazy days on the beach. There was no way I'd ever be able to look at her again. I'd never be able to speak to her, walk past her, or listen to her advice. She was dead to me.

I could only see her now as the woman who took my place— the woman who had lain in bed next to my husband the night before. The woman who made him feel like there was something better out there than me.

She was the girl I'd been trying to picture in my head for months—the tall blond bimbo or my short, brown-haired look-a-like. Except now I no longer had to guess. She was there; she had been there, right in front of me for weeks. Nothing at all like I thought she would be, but possibly it was better that way.

She was a teacher, a woman with a good head on her shoulders with a bright outlook on life. At least she had something to be desired. I don't quite understand it myself, but in a way it made me feel a little better. I'd spent many months agonizing over this situation, constantly comparing myself to whoever she might be. Her looks, her job, her life; and if it didn't even compare, didn't come close to what I had to give, well, that would have made me feel worse. At least if she was better looking than me, I could understand. And I did. I saw what Chase saw in her. She was more than just a pretty face. But what I couldn't see was the answer I'd wanted all along. Why? Why was she better than me? What did she have that Chase couldn't get from me? I thought I was the one. I was the one he had chosen, the finger he put that ring on. If I was enough then; why wasn't I enough now? I wanted the answers to those questions; I just didn't know if I was ready to actually hear them.

Chapter 21

There were several missed calls on my phone by the time I got out of the shower—both from Meghan and Chase. I wondered if they were still together. What had he said to her, and what was her reaction? Did he tell her that his marriage had been over for a long time? Did he explain his way out of the lies he'd told her? I wondered if she'd forgive him; if she'd understand and take him back, or if she'd stick by her no-second-chances rule.

I sat on the bed, wrapped in my towel, staring at my phone. I wanted to call them back. Mostly I wanted to call Meghan. I needed to hear about her relationship with Chase. I needed to hear the things he would say to her, how he acted around her, and if he ever mentioned having a wife. Although I'd known from the stories she told me, he didn't seem to be honest with her either; but I thought maybe something she'd say would give me some insight into why he did this.

Against my better judgment, I hit the call back key. I heard it click and knew she answered, but it took awhile for her to speak.

"I'm sorry." Her voice shook. She swore up and down that she had no idea he was even married, let alone to me. I believed her, I really did, but that didn't make the situation any easier. It didn't make me hate her any less.

I didn't make any small talk. I didn't even acknowledge the words that were coming out of her mouth. I interrupted her explanation by asking if he was still there.

"No, he's gone."

"I think we need to talk. There are things I need to know."

She agreed. Since I was in no condition to be seen in public, I told her to come over. The conversation was cold. There was no emotion inside me. No more hatred, no more sadness, and certainly no love. Once we'd confirmed she was on her way, I hung up.

Meghan knocked and with a half smile on her face, she waved through the glass. I couldn't bring myself to wave back or let her in. She sat down in one of the chairs on the deck. I unlocked the door and went out. I stood on the opposite side of the deck and placed my hands on the railing, leaning on it for support.

We both stared straight ahead for quite some time. I could see her out of the corner of my eye. Her right leg crossed over her left, bouncing up and down with anticipation of what might be to come. She was still wearing what she had on this morning. A pair of gray sweat shorts and a pink cotton t-shirt. She had pulled her hair back into a ponytail, and I could see the mascara stained along her cheek.

"Where did he go?" I asked.

She looked up at me, but didn't say anything. She just shrugged her shoulders as tears glistened in her eyes. Finally, she spoke. "I started screaming at him after awhile. I don't even really remember what I said. He had nothing to say back. He just stared after you with his back to me." She told me how she sat there, in that chair on the deck of her beach house after I had left. Neither of them could look at

107

each other, nor even speak for that matter. Her hand never left her mouth. He stood on the beach where I had left him and watched me run from sight.

Meghan had remembered walking down the deck, grabbing his arm and turning him towards her, and asking him why. Why her: why me? At first, all he could mutter was the dreadful words, *I don't know,* but she told him that wasn't good enough. That she wanted an explanation, and he wasn't leaving until he gave her one. He told her that life as a lawyer had become more stressful than ever, and it got to be too much putting on the charade, and he couldn't handle it all. He needed an escape. He didn't know what kind of escape until he met her. That she made his life less complicated. She didn't expect as much from him as the firm and myself. She saw tears in his eyes, but told him he had no right to cry.

I listened as Meghan continued. My mind drifted to the two of them at her beach house, and it was almost as if I were right there.

"You're a married man! Why put a ring on someone's finger if you aren't going to stand by your promise?" She said he didn't answer. "That's it? You've got nothing to say? You ruined people's lives and you've got nothing to say?"

"That's what I came here to talk to you about. My life, it's been complicated the last few months. I was confused, lost, and completely overwhelmed." Chase said to her.

"That's your excuse? You tear people's hearts into pieces because you're confused?" She screamed.

"I made a mistake, Meghan. I'm sorry. I've had a lot of time to think about things the last couple of weeks. About my life and my marriage. I came here this weekend to tell you everything. And to tell you I can't do this anymore."

"Is that what I was? A mistake?" A tear rolled down the side of her face.

"No, you were not a mistake. Everything I ever said to you I meant. I really do care about you Meghan, but…"

"But what?" Her lip trembled.

"I love my wife."

"Well, now I understand why you didn't make love to me last night. It wasn't because you were tired. It's because for the first time you actually felt guilty about what you were doing. You make me sick."

"Meghan, I really am sorry." He tried to go on, but she cut him off.

"I want you to get your stuff, and get the hell out of my house."

There was no argument from Chase. He went back into the house, and as quickly as he had come, was gone.

With that, I brought myself back into reality.

"I don't know where he is now, and I'm sorry, but I honestly don't care." Meghan looked at me with a sense of intent. "And I know you hate me right now, but I swear to you I had no idea he was married."

"I believe you."

As she explained it all, it started to make sense. "He and his friend, they came into The Pier Shack a few months ago. There was just something about him, I felt immediately drawn to him. There was no ring on his hand that night. If there was, I never would've started any type of conversation with him. You need to know that. I'm not that type of girl."

"I do know that." I moved closer towards her, sliding my hands along the deck railing.

"He never really told me where he was from or what he did. He joked around a lot with me that if I stuck around long enough maybe I'd find out. I think that was maybe why I liked him so much from the start; he was intriguing. My family had started to become suspicious of his long absences and the fact that he would want to meet just the two of us, any place other than here at Kettlewood Island. I had to think of something, so I made up this stupid story about him owning a bunch of stores around the East Coast, and that he'd fly me to where he was from time to time so I could see what it was he did. I always felt awful lying to them, but I knew they'd just give me a hard time. I knew none of it made sense, and I can't really explain it: I enjoyed the thrill. However, this weekend, this time, I'd hoped it would lead to more. I'd been building it up in my mind for weeks, since our last meeting, hoping the talk he wanted to have was that he was ready for more."

"And he wasn't?" I knew from what she told me about their argument it wasn't, but I needed to hear it again.

"The last time we were together…" She stopped for a second, squirming in her chair.

"It's okay, I need to hear it." I closed my eyes and let out a deep breath, as my grip tightened on the railing.

"The last time we were together, everything was going so well. We spent the whole night just talking and laughing. I really thought this was going somewhere." Her voice cut out.

"Your last meeting…where was it?" I'd asked for one reason and one reason only.

"I drove there just for the day, got a hotel, and left really early the next morning; I had no idea that…"

"Where was it, Meghan?" I demanded.

"We met for drinks one night just a few weekends ago."

"Answer the question." An ominous snarl ripped through my now-clenched teeth.

"In Charlotte."

And there it was. The potent smell of a woman's perfume, the very reason Chase stumbled into our bed in the middle of the night, it wasn't because he and Alex had gotten carried away at a bar that night; it was because while his wife was sleeping in bed—alone—he was out nestled up close to the woman society likes to call his mistress. Intimate getaway weekends were one thing, but bringing this woman into my territory, flaunting her around my town: Chase had some serious balls to be doing that.

Looking back on the events of that day, I asked Meghan if Chase had offered any other explanation for his behavior. She paused, trying to answer the question, but unable to get the words out.

"I really think you should ask Chase."

"Tell me what he said, Meghan."

"I can't."

"Why not?"

"Because, before all of this, you and I were friends; and I think my actions have hurt you enough, I don't want to hurt you anymore." I could tell she meant what she was saying, but I didn't care. After all I had been through, I needed answers; and it was clear from the way lies poured off Chase's tongue like water from a hose, they wouldn't be coming from him.

"Listen Meghan, I'm pretty sure I can't feel any worse than I do right now. I need to know, please?"

She was hesitant. I could tell she blamed herself for my pain, and the mere thought of causing any more to me was devastating. She leaned forward, rubbed her eyes with her hands, and started talking.

Chase had told her his life was spinning of control. That for a while, he thought maybe he just wasn't ready to get married. That the pressure and responsibility of taking care of a family and preparing for children was too much for him. He told her that when he was with her, all of the pressures of the everyday world disappeared. He was tired of being angry all the time, never sleeping, and working his life away. Meghan was his escape.

Before she could finish, I had to know. "Did he tell you he loved you?"

"He told me he cared deeply about what we had."

"That's not what I asked you."

Again she hesitated. "No, he never said that to me."

I'm not sure if that was supposed to make me feel better or not. I was numb. Perhaps though, if I could feel something, I would think it may have given me some sense of relief. That at least something maybe still belonged to me. Looking at Meghan, I could tell she was hurt. I didn't blame her. I knew how charming Chase was, how easy he was to fall for. Her heart was broken, too. Maybe not as bad as mine, but what did it matter? Any broken heart hurts.

"He told me he loved you. That everything was all messed up now, that he didn't know what was going to happen next, but the one thing he did know was that he loved you. And he was going to do whatever he had to do to fix what he broke." She started to cry. No one will ever know how hard that was for me. This woman, this poor innocent woman, who just wanted to believe in love, was crying in front of me, because she was in love with my husband and he broke her heart.

Thinking about all the time she wasted. Time spent getting to know someone who didn't really exist. Falling for someone you could never really have and then finding out all of this. In a split second her life had changed, just like mine. I could feel her pain, and I certainly could see it. The feeling of not being enough for someone, of knowing you would do anything for them and they would not do the same for you. I didn't want to, but I felt bad for her. I wanted to hate her, but I couldn't. I couldn't blame her for what she didn't know.

She sat quietly. Her gaunt face looked as tired as I felt. She stood and walked to the railing, leaning her elbows on it, and pointedly avoided looking at me.

It took all I had in me to do what I did next. I walked over to her as she tried to choke back tears. I placed my hand upon her shoulder. Leaving it there for a while as we both said nothing. It was all I could do to comfort her. The more she tried not to cry, the more I cried. I knew Meghan wasn't responsible for this, and that she was just as much a victim to this as I was. But, as we stood there crying, I knew. The friendship we formed was over. It could never be mended. There was no way to get past this. I lost a great friend that day. As if there wasn't enough to cry about, I cried for that, too.

It wasn't long before my compassion dried up and I pulled away. I brushed away the tears that remained and took a deep breath.

"Thank you for that. I needed it," I said. Staying silent, she nodded. "My emotions are all over the place right now. This is a lot for me to handle, but I appreciate you telling me the truth. It's something I obviously have not been getting lately."

"I understand," she muttered, as she slowly made her way to the stairs. With no goodbye, or even a look back, she made her way down the deck to the beach.

"Meghan," I said loudly, making sure she could hear me. She turned to look at me. "You were a good friend. I appreciate all you did for me; it's just, right now—it's too hard. I hope you know I don't blame you for any of this. I know it wasn't your fault."

"You really are too good for him. You deserve better." With that, she turned again and made her way down the beach. That was the last I ever saw of Meghan. I never spoke to her again.

Chapter 22

I knew what was next for me, as I walked back into the cottage. Relief had washed over me after my talk with Meghan. I was proud of the fact that I could comfort "the other woman," that I was strong enough to thank her for what she had done for me, and forgive her for what she didn't know, no matter how much it hurt. I had fought a few of my demons that day; and now, it was time to face the rest.

Before I gave myself any time to retract, I picked up the phone and dialed his number. When he picked up, I asked him where he was. He said he was wandering the streets of the island, not sure where to go. I could hear the tears in his voice as he spoke, but unlike Meghan I didn't feel sorry for him. He had done this to himself.

"Go home, Chase," I managed to say.

"I can't go home without you, Haylie. I just can't."

I didn't know what to say to that. Did he feel bad because he'd gotten caught? Or did he feel bad because he'd learned his lesson the hard way? Relationships were not always black and white, cut and dry. There is always so much history, so much emotional impact on a life that makes it so hard to just walk away when someone hurts you. But deep inside, I knew I had to stay strong. I couldn't let my emotions get the best of me. It was time to stand my ground, weigh out my options, and choose the path that was best for me. I wasn't going to let anyone tell me otherwise.

"I'm going home, Chase." I said. "But it will be without you. I can't even look at you right now. When I get home, I don't want you there. I'm not ready to deal with you yet."

"Where am I supposed to go, Haylie? A hotel?"

"A hotel, a friend's house, or a cardboard box, Chase. I really don't care right now. That's not my main concern. I just don't want you to be home when I get there. Figure it out."

"Okay, I'll do that for you, but we need to talk about this."

"And when I'm ready, we will. I'll let you know when that is. Until then, leave me alone."

He agreed, and with that I pulled the phone from my ear and started packing. I had been away long enough. It was time to face my reality. No one can run forever. I wanted to move forward. I wanted to smile again, to laugh again. And until I figured all of this out, I knew that wasn't going to happen.

For the rest of the day, I didn't do much. Packing didn't take long, and my appetite had vanished. Just thinking about food made my stomach churn, so wasting time sitting down for a meal was out of the question. Instead, I walked to the end of the beach where the water met the shore. I sat there with my arms wrapped around my knees and stared off into the emptiness in front of me. The serenity of the breeze blowing through my hair calmed my nerves. It gave me a sense of clarity.

I replayed the events of this morning over and over again. Watching Chase on the deck from afar, and the way his face looked when he finally saw me standing there. I saw Meghan, all happy and smiling, walk out the door, and then the devastation in her face when she realized the truth. That was my life. That really happened to me. I had to keep convincing myself, as it seemed so surreal. How could a man look himself in the mirror in the morning and be proud of who he was, knowing he was being untruthful and disloyal to the woman who made him her whole world?

Before all this happened, men having affairs would cross my mind, but I always had the *things like that don't happen to me* mentality. I guess, looking at it now, it seems anything can happen to anyone at any time. No one is immune to anything. Do I really have to be watching my back all the time, always on the defensive? Trusting no one but myself was a cold cross to bear, but at that moment, I wore it. It was time to worry about me.

Chapter 23

The weather the next morning seemed fitting. It was dark and gloomy. Not a hint of sun in the sky. I didn't sleep well the night before, so was up early getting ready for the trip home. I grabbed my belongings, locked up, and returned the key to the rental office.

Before driving out of town, I stopped at the little coffee shop where I had run into Meghan after my first dinner at The Pier Shack. I watched from across the street first, making sure she wasn't there. Then I jogged to the door, hoping she wouldn't make her way in behind me. It seemed I had come during the early morning rush; the line was long when I arrived. I had my guard up the whole time I was standing there, thinking I'd hear her voice at any minute, but I never did. I breathed a sigh of relief as I grabbed my coffee and headed to the car.

It took me a while, once I started it up, to actually put the car in drive. I knew what I would be going home to. I was so strong yesterday, pushing him away, but how strong would I be once I got back to our house? Once I was surrounded by the memories of our life and all we had built. Would I be able to stand my ground? Would I be able to walk away, pick up my life and start over, or would he know just what to say to make me stay? I had no idea what to expect. The constant tug-of-war of emotions made it impossible for me to wonder what choice I even wanted to make; but if I wanted to find out, I had to go. I turned the steering wheel, easing the car into the traffic, and headed towards the highway.

I pulled into my driveway late that afternoon and, sure enough, Chase's car was nowhere to be seen. I didn't grab any of my things from the trunk, just walked inside. It was so dark and quiet. The sun wasn't shining and it made the house so dim. I felt around on the wall and flicked on the lights. Everything seemed to be just the way I had left it. The blanket was still folded up on the middle of the couch with the pillow on top, from the last night I had been here. Peeking into the kitchen, I saw the dishes sitting in the drying rack and the dish-rag on the kitchen counter. I could even see the note I left, sitting right next to it.

I sat on the couch. Fiddling my fingers, I looked around. The vaulted living room ceilings, archways leading into the den to the right of the fireplace; it was the simple charm I loved about this house. The columns that separated the living room from the kitchen, and crown molding that was throughout, gave the house that Southern feeling we had always said we wanted. Yup, we sure had it all.

I glanced over at the fireplace; I could see my reflection in the glass. I looked pale and my eyes were swollen from exhaustion. My hair was a mess. I looked sad. Out of the corner of my eye, I caught a picture atop the mantle. There, I saw a girl I hardly recognized anymore. Her smile stretched from ear to ear and her eyes were bright. Her hair pulled back into a neat and curly side ponytail, holding the hand of the man who made her whole world spin. It was our wedding picture. How blissful we looked that day, as we stood hand in hand. The colors were so crisp and vibrant. It was the epitome of a perfect day. I thought for a moment about Chase's proposal, and the big secret plan he put together all by himself.

On weekends, once I'd graduated college and was working full time, we'd hit the hiking trail and go on short road-trip getaways to local wineries. It became "our thing." Every chance we got, we would visit a new winery, stretching our reach further and further around the state of North Carolina. We would drive for hours some weekends, just to find a new Moscato wine for me, or a Cabernet for him. Life was simple and fun. It just worked with us. Sure we had our disagreements, but fighting was not something we did often.

As the weather grew colder, we spent more time indoors. While I was working late nights in front of the TV creating marketing presentations, Chase worked hard to plan a romantic spring getaway for our two-year anniversary. Being that I was originally from New York, I never really explored much of the Carolinas outside of our winery road trips, and Chase wanted to take me somewhere special. He booked a cute little bed and breakfast in the mountains of western North Carolina. He would read me all types of activities we could do, as we tried to narrow down our choices. I looked forward to it all winter.

By the time spring came, we were both in desperate need of a vacation—me from work and Chase from preparing for the bar exam that was just around the corner. We packed the Jeep and hopped on Interstate 40 for the four-hour drive west.

"This is going to be a great vacation." I clapped my hands

together.

"Yes it is." Chase smiled.

"I think we should make sure we go hiking. I hear this is the best time of the year for it."

He nodded and reached over to pat my thigh. He was quiet most of the drive, lost in his own thoughts. I figured he was nervous, still thinking about taking the bar, so I didn't want to push too much.

After four hours, we reached our bed and breakfast. While Chase unpacked the car, I checked in. A beautiful stone front porch met me at the entrance of the inn. As I walked into the parlor, I could see a wood-burning fireplace—what a charming place. The Victorian inspiration was breathtaking.

When I arrived at the front desk, a silver-haired woman with a warm smile stood behind it.

"Welcome to the Misty Trail Bed and Breakfast. How can I help you?"

"I'm checking in. Last name is Julian."

"Yes, you've reserved the Blue Ridge Suite for three nights. Here are your keys and there is a welcome basket in the room. You'll also find brochures to the many attractions we have around here."

As I grabbed the keys, Chase snuck up behind me with our luggage and we made our way up to the third floor. The room was gorgeous. There was a glass chandelier dangling elegantly in the foyer above us as we walked in, and the French countryside décor made us feel like we were thousands of miles from reality.

We woke early the next morning to get ready for our visit to one of the popular, historic estates in the area. We took a private carriage ride around the gardens, toured the winery, and dined at the estate's only restaurant. It had been a perfect day. I was about to be very surprised, though, at just how much more perfect it was going to get.

When we got back to our suite, I kicked off my shoes and fell onto the bed. Chase lay down beside me. We didn't say a word for some time. My head rested on his chest and his hand caressed my arm.

"I think you could use a hot bath." Startling me, he sat up. "I'll order some room service and you can take a bath while we wait for it."

"Well I certainly won't argue with that. My feet are aching after walking all day. The thought of relaxing in the deep soaking tub is very appealing right now."

"Great. I'll get the water ready." He headed into the bathroom.

I undressed and when it was ready, slid into the tub.

"Want to join me?" I asked, thinking it might help clear his mind.

"I'm going to order us some dinner. This is your night to relax."

"Alright, well you know where to find me if you change your mind."

I was in the bath for about twenty minutes when I heard a knock on the outside door. Chase's voice echoed through the walls as he thanked the man for our food. I shouted from the bathroom, asking if it was time to eat. He told me it wasn't ready yet and to stay in there until he came to get me out. I was almost a prune by the time he walked into the bathroom.

"Everything is all set. You have to keep your eyes closed

though, when you walk out. You promise?" he asked. "Only open them when I tell you to."

"Alright, I promise."

I stepped into the towel he held up for me and dried myself off. Once I was dressed in the camisole he handed me, I threw my hair back in a damp ponytail, eager to see what my surprise was. With his hands over my eyes, Chase guided me into the main room. He left me standing there for just a minute, until he said, "Okay, open them."

I gasped. Candles flickered on the table, illuminating silver cutlery and a gourmet dinner. Chase was in front of me, down on one knee, with a ring box in his hand. I slapped both hands over my mouth.

"I've been thinking about the future a lot lately; and every time I do, I see you in it. A year from now, five years from now, even twenty years from now, I see you by my side. You're everything I could have ever wanted in a wife, and I want to spend forever with you." His voice began to shake and I could see him fighting to hold back tears in those blue eyes. He opened the ring box. "Haylie, will you marry me?"

I stared at the open-curved diamond platinum band in envy. It held in place a perfect 2-carat solitaire diamond. I could feel tears forming as I blurted out my answer.

"Yes! Yes, I'll marry you!"

I bent over, placed my hands gently on his cheeks and kissed him. As he stood up, I wrapped my arms around his neck and squeezed him as tightly as I could.

"You have to let go so I can put this on." He was staring into my eyes.

"Oh right, yes!" I giggled and put my hand out as he slipped the ring on my finger. It was absolutely stunning, and fit perfectly! I had waited my whole life for this, and couldn't have asked for anything better.

I stared at that picture for a very long while, remembering just how happy we were that day. Thanks to my love of Reese Witherspoon, and *Sweet Home Alabama*, we were married on a crisp fall day at a plantation just like the one in the movie. I walked down the aisle with a mixture of peach and white roses in my hand. We danced the night away with our family and friends.

And now, it had all come to this. Sitting alone on the couch in our living room, wondering how in the world we got here. Two people, so young and in love, with the whole world at our fingertips. And now, here we were, all our hopes, dreams, and plans crushed. I stood up slowly and walked to the fireplace, never taking my eyes off the photo. I slid my finger over the glass of the frame a few times where his face was. Then gripped my fingers tightly around the frame. I pulled it into my chest for a minute, closed my eyes and envisioned the very moment that was captured. Then, I threw it.

It flew across the living room before it hit the wall near the front door. I heard the impact and watched the glass shatter. All the worrying I'd been doing, the constant anxiety, it had finally become too much. You can only bend something so much until it breaks and that is what happened to me. I turned back to the fireplace, swept my arms across the mantle, and flung the rest of the pictures to the floor. I picked up our wedding album from the coffee table, its weight satisfying, and threw it. The books that rested on the other side of it, I picked them up and hurled those as well. The loud thumps as they hit the wall punctuated my screams.

By the time I was done, my living room was a train wreck. Nothing but broken glass and clutter surrounded me. It was like I had blacked out. I couldn't stop myself, and when I was done I couldn't remember doing it. I stood in the middle of the mess for some time; the only sound was that of my ragged breathing. I wiped sweat from my brow, and my shoulders slumped. And then, when I was ready, just like I had to do with the mess my life had become, I grabbed a broom; and as I started the massive job of cleaning up, the tears came anew.

It took me over an hour to make sure all the glass had been picked up off the floor. I swept multiple times, vacuumed, and mopped. I threw everything in a garbage bag, ripping up the pictures as I pulled them off the floor. It made me feel better. At that moment, I couldn't look at his face.

Chapter 24

Several days passed since I had my outburst in the living room. I didn't do much in that time. I left once to go to the grocery store. Hoping to avoid anyone I knew, I went to a store in the next town over. I spent most nights on the couch, watching soap opera re-runs with a box of tissues in my lap. I hadn't worked up the courage to call Chase. Sometimes it bothered me, wondering what he was doing, and if he was hurting as bad as I was; but other times, I tried not to care.

It was just after dinnertime late that next Friday, when I heard a knock on my door. I was caught off-guard. My friends and family were still completely unaware of the situation, and I planned on keeping it that way until I was ready to make a final decision. I hesitated—what if it was Chase?

I smoothed my clothes and made my way through the living room. Peering through the peephole, I could see Katie. I'd felt awful— I hadn't called her during any of this. She'd texted me several times. I always meant to respond, but would get sidetracked and forget. I opened the door and stood aside. As soon as she stepped over the threshold she hugged me, then leaned back and squeezed my shoulders with a sympathetic look on her face.

"Can I get you something to drink?" I asked, trying to break the awkward silence.

"No thanks. I just came over to see how you were doing. I hadn't heard from you in a while."

"I'm sorry. I...I just didn't want to talk about it. Do you want to sit down?" She followed me to the couch. "Have you spoken to Chase recently?"

"No. Have you?"

"No, not in awhile."

As Katie was one of the very few people who sort of knew what was going on, I began to fill her in. I told her how, after the credit card statements, I continued to look through Chase's things and came across the video; and after seeing that, I could no longer be in the house with him, so I left. I told her how I found the airline receipt and knew he would be on Kettlewood Island for the holiday weekend, so that's where I went.

I explained how I was befriended by Meghan, how close we had become, how spending time with her helped ease the pain and put my life into perspective. And of course, I ended the story with finding Chase outside her beach house that morning and all the details that followed. She didn't say anything once I finished. She sat there, her hand resting on mine. Then, with no warning, she began to cry. Quickly it turned into a sob. I kept telling her I would be okay and not to feel sorry for me. After a few minutes, she had calmed down and looked at me. Her serious face worried me.

"I've been thinking a lot about how I didn't stick up for you with the girls when you came to us for support, but there was a reason I couldn't say anything; if I did, I would have been a fraud. I mean, any good friend would tell you to leave him, that he doesn't deserve you, but I can't do that."

"Huh? What are you talking about?"

"The last time you came over, you kept mentioning how you wished your relationship could be easy like mine and David's, how we were always happy together, and I just couldn't bring myself to tell you." She looked at the ground. I put my hand on top of hers, reassuring her that whatever it was she wanted to tell me, I was here. "Three years ago, Dave and I were going through a real rough patch. We fought all the time about him always being gone, forgetting our plans, and just treating me more like his maid than his wife. He was always making demands of me and I began to feel alone." The tears were still in her eyes. She told me about how she reconnected with an old flame during that time and reached out to him for support and someone to talk to. "It was innocent at first. I just needed to feel wanted." I could tell it wasn't easy for her to go on, but she did. She told me how hours of talking over dinner and drinks one night turned into something more. "It was just one time. One time that I've regretted every day since." Dave most likely would have never found out what happened, but Katie couldn't live with that. The night he arrived home from his business trip, she told him. She told him that she felt lonely and unappreciated and that there was no excuse for what she had done, but that it happened. He flipped out on her, called her every name in the book, and threw her out of the house. "At first, he told me never to come back again unless it was to pick up my stuff, but after a few days he wanted to talk."

They sat down for hours and yelled and screamed at each

other. She told me that she will never forgive herself for what she had done, but it made her realize how important Dave was to her. How much she wanted Dave to love her—and it made Dave painfully aware of the way he'd been treating her. I could tell she was still in pain from what she'd done, that she didn't want to justify the things that happened to me, but she wanted me to know that I had a choice if I wanted one.

"I can't speak for Chase, but I've never been sorrier about anything in my entire life; and there's no excuse for what I did, but I'm thankful that Dave gave me another chance. I'm thankful he saw my remorse and my pain and that we could work it out."

I searched for something to say, "Oh. Wow, um." I took a deep breath, "Thanks for sharing. I know that couldn't have been easy."

I told her about destroying everything in the house. How, if I had it in me, I would just forgive and move on, but I wasn't sure I could. Nodding, Katie listened as I went back and forth about each choice I could make. It was nice to be able to have someone caring to tell.

When I was done, Katie assured me that whatever decision I made, she knew it would be the best one for me. "I'm just next door. If you need anything, you come on over, okay?"

"Thank you. It's nice to know I'm not alone."

Once she left, I knew it was time to make a decision. I had put it off long enough. I knew Chase wanted to come over and talk, but up until then I wasn't ready. One minute I was throwing things and destroying memories, the next I was crying, telling myself that no one was perfect and that I owed it to our marriage to give him another chance. That would once again switch when I would think about the video I saw, the credit card statement, and the fact that he drove 4 hours to see another woman—knowing his wife was in pain, and hurting without him. During those moments, I hated him again. I wanted to pack all of his things and throw them out on the front porch, lock the doors, and tell him to come over and pick it all up and never come back.

All of the thinking I did that night and the several days after, all the emotions I dealt with, were extremely draining. I didn't want to live in this in-between space anymore. There was no more avoiding it. It was time to talk to Chase.

I jumped in the shower, which I hadn't done in several days, and tried to make myself look like something other than death. Then, I picked up the phone and dialed those seven numbers I had known by heart for the last several years. The phone barely made it to my ear before he picked it up. He told me his phone hadn't left his side, hoping at any moment I would call.

"I'm ready," I said. He knew exactly what I meant.

"I can be there in ten minutes, if that's okay?"

"Okay, I'll see you then." I hung up without saying goodbye. Breathing deeply, I prepared myself for what I was about to face.

Chapter 25

I swear I could see eyes peeking between the blinds of every window on the block when Chase's car finally pulled in the driveway. I could imagine each of those women that I, at one time, called my friend, on the phone with each other gossiping about it and how they told me I should have just left it alone.

I'm sure their eyes were fixated on him, from the moment he emerged from the car all the way to the front door. I heard his footsteps come up the porch, then suddenly stop. At first I thought he would knock, so I waited. When moments passed and I hadn't heard anything, I knew he was doing the same thing I was: preparing himself. It seemed like an eternity that I sat there, waiting for him to make any move. Slowly the door handle began to turn. As it opened, my heart began to beat rapidly. This was the first time since that horrible day on the beach that I had seen Chase. Mixed emotions flooded through me as he closed the door behind him.

I sat on the oversized chair in the living room. I didn't want to sit on the couch and have him sit next to me. I stared at the floor as he walked in. He maneuvered around the furniture, but I didn't look up. He sat down, leaned forward, and folded his hands in between his legs. He was looking right at me, I could tell, but my eyes looked in every direction but his.

I sat there waiting. Neither of us spoke. I hated to have to be the one to speak first. This was not my fault. We were not here because of what I had done. He slid further to the right of the couch, making his way closer to me, just like I knew he would. At least I had the chair arm as a barrier; he couldn't get any closer. The silence became deafening. I couldn't handle it anymore, as he sat there with a pitiful look on his face.

"Well, you're the one who wanted to talk. I'm waiting." I ground out through clenched teeth.

"I'm sorry." Finally, he spoke—just two words. Two words he thought would make everything all right. I repeated them back to him, hoping he would understand how ridiculous they sounded.

"I'm sorry. That's all you have to say? Tell me, Chase, what exactly are you sorry for?" I couldn't help it; I didn't wait to hear his answer. "Sorry for throwing away our marriage, eight years of our lives, lying to me? Or are you just sorry that I found out?"

I could tell that he knew nothing he would say was going to make this any better, but he was going to give it all he had. He stirred in his seat as he gathered his thoughts.

"For everything. For hurting you, for lying to you. All of it. If I could take it back, I would." The words stumbled out of his mouth through his tear-soaked lips.

"But you can't." I jumped up, and paced around the room. "You can't take it back. You ruined everything. Do you even know how hard it is to just look at you right now? All of those thing you did with her. How could you?"

132

"I know." His voice quivered as I interrupted him.

"No, you don't. You don't know. All those nights I went to bed alone. All those times I sat here crying. My life has been miserable these last few months. I didn't even want to wake up in the morning."

"Haylie, I'm so sorry. I'm going to fix this, okay? Whatever happened, it was wrong. I know that and it will never ever happen again. I love you so much."

"You love me? Really? You have one hell of a way of showing it, Chase. If I hadn't found out, this would all probably still be going on."

"No, it wouldn't. I went to Kettlewood Island to end it with her. When you left, I realized what a mess I'd made. That I was running from a life I should've been thankful for. I just got so caught up in the stress and the pressure that I cracked. But I see now that nothing, Haylie, *nothing* in this world is worth losing you over."

He walked towards me and reached out to place his hands on my arms. I lifted my hands to stop him, as I backed away. He was sorry, he loved me, and he couldn't take it if he lost me. That was everything I thought I wanted to hear. Those were the words I thought were going to put everything back together again: but they didn't. I was hurt, angry, and lost. I couldn't look at my husband without feeling pain. I didn't want him to touch me, or hold me, or comfort me. The security, happiness, and comfort I once felt in his embrace were gone. He stood there, waiting for me to say something, anything that would let him know we still had a chance.

"I can't lose you, Haylie. You are everything to me."

"Oh, so suddenly you had a change in conscience. Is that it?"

"I made a mistake. I let all my fears of failing and not being good enough take over, and I made a mistake. Everything happened so fast. I turned into someone I didn't recognize anymore, and I did a lot of things I'm not proud of. I know I can't take them back, but that's all it was, Haylie; a mistake. It's over now, but you and me, we have so much history, so much to look forward to. I need you to forgive me. I need you to tell me we can fix this."

His voice trailed off. He lowered his head and brushed the sides of it with his hands. The tears were flowing now like rivers down his face. The strong, bold man I married, who never showed any signs of weakness, was actually crying.

I thought the day I saw him out on Meghan's deck was the hardest thing I'd ever have to experience, but I was wrong. Watching Chase cry was excruciatingly hard for me. It wasn't because I felt sorry for him, but because of the inner struggle it created inside of me. I so badly wanted to grab him, pull him in and hold him, tell him everything was going to be okay. But the truth was, I had my doubts about how genuine those tears were. He had been so manipulative, had lied so many times, those tears could have all been part of this new persona to reel me back in. It was so sad, not trusting the man I loved. I fought with everything in me not to move from where I was now standing, not to share his tears.

"I'm your wife. You should have come to me. When have I ever not been there to help you?" He shook his head, telling me there never was a time, which made his story that much worse. I would have done anything for that man, and he knew it. "Calling her is one thing, Chase, but sleeping with her: that is unforgivable." I thought about how Meghan had said she'd met with her mystery man on more than a few occasions. My whole body shivered at how, after every one, he would come home to me, kiss me, and touch me like it was nothing at all.

"You don't make the same mistake twice, Chase. After the first time, it was no longer a mistake. It was a conscious decision to betray your wife, the vows you made, and the life we had together."

Through his tears, he managed to speak his plea.

"I'm so sorry for all of it. If I could take it back, I would. I swear. I love you so much, Haylie. If you just give me another chance, I promise you I'll be the husband you've always wanted. I won't ever let you down again. Just let me prove it to you."

"Tell me something, Chase. Did you think you'd get away with it?"

"I don't know what I thought, Haylie. I obviously wasn't thinking at all."

Love is a funny thing. It can make you the happiest person in the whole world when it's good; but when it all goes bad, it can crush you beyond recognition. We sat there for a long time, me trying to figure out what to say, and him hoping they would be the words he wanted to hear.

Tears welled up in my eyes. The words he was saying, the pleas he was making—I knew for me it would never be enough. My faith in him was shattered. Never would I be able to look at him the same way again. I'd always wonder when he went out where he was, and who he was with. My insides would be crawling with anxiety every time he wasn't near me. I couldn't live like that. I know my vows said for better or for worse, and I know this was certainly the worst, but I knew in my heart that I would never be able to forgive, forget, and move on. I knew every night he wrapped his arms around me I'd wonder if he wished it was her. Every time the phone would ring, I knew my heart would pound at the thought of who it might be. I wasn't prepared to do that for the rest of my life.

It was the first time since my suspicions had begun that I admitted those words to myself. It was starting to become clear to me. For so long, I had wondered how we would move on, how I would ever get past this, and if our love could withstand it all; but in that moment, looking at him face to face, my heart finally spoke the truth. Every woman has a line in their relationship. It may be imaginary, but it's there. Every woman's line is different. Some actions may weigh heavier on one person than another, but in the end it's all the same. Cross that line and the consequences can be life-changing and devastating. It's the type of line where, once you cross it, you can never go back. Chase knew, based on my stories about that high school boyfriend who broke every ounce of innocent trust I had as a teenager, where my line had been drawn; and like it or not, he had crossed it.

"Things get tough, Chase, that's the way life is. But when it does, you don't just go running away from it all into the arms of the first girl willing to go to bed with you. That's not how it works. A marriage is supposed to be forever. You made a promise to me, and you broke it. This wasn't just a one-time thing; you saw her over and over and just lied to my face like I was nobody."

He tried to interrupt, but I was on a roll and knew if I let him speak, I may lose the courage to say what it was I needed to say.

Finally, I said what it was he was waiting for—the answer to his plea.

"You can never take away the memories I have of us; I will hold those deep inside. And someday, when my heart heals, I may even be able to forgive you. But I just don't have it in me for second chances. I've given those before and they always turn into third or fourth chances. It never ends."

"Not me, Haylie. It's gonna be different this time. I'm done. No more. Just let me show you; you owe me that much."

My mind flashed back to that day in the park when our relationship first became official. How he had spoken those words to me as we sat on the bench waiting for the sun to go down, vowing he would never be like those who came before him. Assuring me that, if I agreed to be his girlfriend, I would never feel that kind of pain again. And the night he proposed: while we lay in bed, he promised he would spend the rest of his life doing everything he could to make me as happy as I had made him.

"I owe you nothing." I shook my head. "I gave you everything, and you took it all away."

Chase knew how important loyalty and honesty were to me. He knew it was a deal-breaker for me. He had made me a promise he couldn't keep. I couldn't forgive and forget something like that. Now it was my turn to say those two dreaded words.

"I'm sorry, Chase, but I just can't. I can't get past this, I don't have it in me. You and me, what we had, the life we built, it's over. I'm done." That's all I could manage to get out without my voice wavering. I wanted him to know I meant it, that there was no changing my mind.

He nodded as his lips trembled. I told him to give me a few

days to pack my things and he could have *his* house back. It was my way of twisting the knife a little deeper, even though there were no words that could hurt him as much as his actions had hurt me. He fought me for a little bit, telling me I could have the house, how he ruined everything and he didn't deserve anything; but I didn't want it.

I wanted to prove to myself that I was going to be okay without him. That I could stand on my own two feet and make my own life, and be just fine. Picking up and starting over on my own was what I needed to do for me. I declined his offer, but we agreed I could stay in the house until everything was finalized. So that was it. My marriage was over.

Chapter 26

During the months it took to prepare the terms of the divorce, I shared the news with my family and friends from back home, who were completely blindsided. My mom cried, my friends swore up and down and called him words too vulgar to repeat, and my brother and father thought through every version of pain and suffering for him they could think of. I promised all of them that I was fine.

Once the divorce proceedings began, it felt like a million pounds had been lifted off of me. Suddenly, I didn't have to wonder where Chase was, or who he was talking to. I did wonder how he was doing from time to time, but the anxiety that he and Meghan had created had completely disappeared.

By the time my lawyer's office called me to come in and sign the final papers, all of my stuff had pretty much been moved into my new apartment. There were only a couple of boxes that would be able to fit in my car on the final trip from Oak Creek. My family came down to help, and they were planning on staying a while, until I was settled in. Chase didn't come anywhere around the house once they arrived. He'd text me every now and then, but I'd only respond to the ones that were relative to the situation. I chose to ignore the *I miss you* and *I'm sorry* texts, as it wouldn't do any good for either of us. It was hard at first. I was so used to the life I was living that having to just pick up and go was quite an adjustment. Pretending someone didn't exist was hard.

The divorce took about a year to be finalized. We had agreed upon everything during the settlement, so there wasn't anything to contest. I didn't ask for much. Just my stake in the house and a few pieces of furniture I knew he could do without. For the most part, I didn't want anything that reminded me of what could have been, so once I put my deposit down on a chic new industrial-looking loft apartment in uptown Charlotte, I went on an IKEA shopping spree.

I traded the suburbs for the city life. One entire wall of my new loft was lined with windows. I enjoyed a pristine city view, and I made sure to have two bedrooms for visitors. Mostly, though, to be sure I had enough closet space for my shoe and purse collections. To try and curb the loneliness, I went out on a whim and rescued a dog from a local animal shelter. He was the cutest little eight-week-old mutt I'd ever seen. They didn't know exactly what breed he was, but I guessed he had a little lab in him. I named him Marcus. During the whole process, he certainly kept my mind from always wandering to my troubles.

I left Marcus at the apartment with my family, during what would be my final visit to the house in Oak Creek to collect the last couple of boxes. I did a final sweep of the house by myself. My mom insisted on coming with me, but I needed this time alone. I walked through each room, saying goodbye to the memories that were made in each one. I knew it wasn't going to be easy, building a life by myself, starting over, and opening myself up to the possibility of love again.

But I knew I had made the right decision. I knew that I wanted to feel secure in a relationship, and I just wasn't ever going to feel that with Chase again.

I think I stood in the living room the longest. That was the place Chase and I stood when we first uttered the words, "this is our house." We were so excited the first time our realtor took us here. We had gone through so many open houses and nothing had felt like home. Then we walked into this beautiful white colonial at 12572 Cherry Blossom Court, and we just knew it was the one. Chase threw his arms around me and pulled me in closely, as confirmation that we both agreed. I could still see us as we spent much of that afternoon walking into each room just like I was doing at that moment, except back then we were planning where the furniture would be placed and what colors we would paint the walls.

Most of the furniture was still as it had been, but the feeling just wasn't the same. I no longer felt like I belonged there. All the work I had put into making it a home was for naught; all the dreams I had hoped to build in it had disappeared.

When I finished, I placed the key on the ebony-colored bench that sat just inside the front door. Looking at my left hand, I realized something I hadn't in the last few months. I was still wearing my wedding ring. I slid it off of my finger and let it rest between my thumb and index finger as I admired it. It really was a beautiful ring. I remember, during the weeks that followed our engagement, I used to stare at it for hours.

Looking at it now, it shined just as brightly as it did that day. I thought about putting it back on my finger, or placing it in the pocket of my purse until I found a place for it later, but what did I need it for? That ring symbolized something that didn't exist anymore. It symbolized a lifetime commitment. It meant that two people destined to be together had found each other, and that they would lean on each other through the good and the bad. That ring was the sign of a promise, never meant to be broken; but it had been. I didn't need to be reminded of all those things, so I bent back down and placed the ring gently next to the key. Leaving it behind meant there was hope I could move on.

I turned off the light and closed the door for the final time. As I walked down the porch steps, Chase was pulling into the driveway. Of all days, he had gotten home from work early. He pulled his car up next to mine and stepped out.

"I didn't think you'd still be here."

"Just saying my goodbyes." I said.

He nodded. "I really am sorry. For all of this."

"I know you are. If only sorry was enough." Pausing for a moment, I stared at the driveway. "I should get going."

"It was good to see you."

"Goodbye, Chase." I got into the car, placed the final box of my things in the passenger's seat and closed the door.

He watched me back out of the driveway and turn onto the road before he headed inside. I looked into the rearview mirror, and for the first time in a long time, I saw a girl who had hope.

I felt a smile graze my face. I had closed a huge chapter in my life and was about to embark on another.

"You're going to be just fine, Haylie. It's all going to be okay,"

I said as I pulled away.

You see, in every story, it's not about the ending. It's about the chapters in the middle and how you make it through them; but we all know how important it is to get through them, in order to get to see how it ends. While you're going through them, it might be scary— terrifying actually—but you'll learn so much about yourself at the end of each one. During this entire process, I surprised myself by how strong I really was. I had done something I never thought was possible. I stood up for what I'd believed in, and walked away from something that wasn't good enough, because I knew I deserved better. It was going to be a long, hard road; but I was ready.

I turned on the radio and one of my favorite songs was on. *"Don't Stop Believin'"* by Journey. I sang along to the lyrics and adjusted the rear-view mirror, so I could no longer see the house I once called home. There would be no more looking back. From now on, I was looking only to the future, and I was ready to take on whatever it was that would be waiting for me.

About the Author

Courtney Giardina was born and raised just outside of Rochester, NY, where she spent most of her childhood playing many different sports before she focused on her love for gymnastics and cheerleading. As she tumbled and chanted her way through high school, she also coached young girls who held the same passion.

She graduated with a Bachelor's degree in Business Marketing from Marist College. After college, Courtney spent some time in the entertainment industry as a backup dancer and also acting in indie films.

In 2012, Courtney moved to Charlotte, NC and has been focusing on finally doing all the things she said she would do "someday," including pursuing her acting career and writing that book she always talked about. After making a New Year's resolution to write her first novel, Courtney completed *Tear Stained Beaches* after nine months of long nights and wearing out the delete button on her keyboard.

When she's not busy writing her next novel, Courtney enjoys working out, traveling, and spending time with those she loves. She resides in Charlotte with her dog, DJ and her cat, Neeko.

Author Q&A

Favorite scene in Tear Stained Beaches?

Hmmm, there are quite a few I love because they are powerful. I'd have to say, though, the scene in Tear Stained Beaches that I really love is the coffee shop scene. I can't help but laugh every time I read it. I don't want to give too much detail and spoil the fun for those who haven't read it yet, but it's hilarious. A very light-hearted moment in the book where you get to see the real personalities of Haylie and Chase.

Do you have another novel currently in the works?

I do! I'm currently about 20,000 words in. I'm not sure how far into it that means, since my characters keep challenging me to go in all sorts of directions with the storyline. I guess we shall see how it turns out!

Is it a sequel to Tear Stained Beaches?

It's not a sequel, but you will get a little sneak peek into Haylie's life after Chase in the new novel.

What do you do in your spare time?

I love to work out. I just recently took up boxing and I love it. I find new ways to challenge myself each time I go. I'm also a very outdoorsy person. Hiking, boating, or just laying by the pool are all places you can find me when the sun is out.

Does Prince Charming Exist?

I'd like to think there is someone out there for everyone. Though, if he was easy to find, I don't think we'd appreciate him as much.

What is one thing you spend too much money on?

Makeup

Name something you aren't particularly good at, but wish you were?

Singing. Since I do it all the time—in the Jeep, shower and throughout the day in my apartment—it would be nice if I could do it well.

What is your favorite part about being a writer?
The amazing people I've met along the way. I am part of a few author groups on Facebook and the support, guidance, and advice I receive from those in it has been invaluable. I've also come across other writers and editors on Twitter who I keep in contact with regularly. They are always willing to lend a hand wherever I need. This is such a supportive industry, and I'm proud to be a part of it.

Anything you'd like to say to your readers out there?
Just a big "Thank You." You will never know how truly appreciative I am for your continued support. For reading Tear Stained Beaches, sharing it with your friends, and also letting me know your thoughts on it. Your kind words have meant everything to me and continue to inspire me to keep writing.

Book Club Discussion Questions

1. Haylie heads to a small beach town to get away and try to think more clearly. What happens when you get out of your regular surroundings? Would that make it easier or harder to make an important decision?

2. Throughout the novel, readers go on a rollercoaster of emotions with Haylie. What do you think about Chase? Do you hate him or feel sorry for him?

3. Haylie is shocked when her friends insist she keep her findings about Chase's affair to herself and try to forget about it. What would you do if you felt really strongly about something, and one of your most trusted friends told you to do the opposite of what you thought you should do?

4. What do you think was the most heartbreaking part of the book?

5. In support of Chase's ambitions, Haylie leaves a job she loves to relocate to Charlotte. What do you think is more important? Having your own career or supporting the one you love? Have you, or would you, ever give up your career for someone else's happiness?

6. If there was a second novel about Haylie, what would you like to see happen to her?

7. If you were Haylie, would you have stayed in Charlotte after leaving Chase, or started over somewhere else? Would you consider Charlotte to be full of sad memories and heartbreak, or unlimited new potential?

8. Haylie describes her perfect "Sweet Home Alabama" wedding on a Southern estate. If money were no object, describe the details of your dream wedding. If you've already had a wedding, was it the event of your dreams, or would you have done something differently?

9. Did the book end the way you expected it to? Would you have made a different choice?

10. What did you think about how Haylie handled the situation with Meghan, both at the discovery of her relationship with Chase and then back at Haylie's beach house?

11. As Haylie says goodbye to the house one last time, she leaves her ring on the bench, stating that it represented a promise that didn't exist anymore. Do you think people are obligated to give back wedding or engagement rings if things don't work out? Does it depend on whether the relationship ends poorly or on civil terms?

12. Do you think Meghan would have stayed with Chase if he hadn't decided to end things and try and fix things with Haylie?

About Take Two Publishing

Take Two Publishing is dedicated to partnering with talented novelists and expanding the reach of their audience by providing an unparalleled publishing service. We maintain an intimate environment in order to give each author the exclusive attention they deserve. *Take Two* places a sincere interest in the success of each author. We strive to publish high quality novels that readers won't want to put down, and also utilize the best social media marketing techniques to spread the word.

Submissions

Take Two Publishing is always looking for new and exciting stories. We publish books that are so good we lose sleep because we just can't put them down. If you believe your story meets our submission guidelines, we'd love to hear from you!

We are looking for fresh fiction that features **compelling female characters**. Whether we love them, hate them, or change our minds halfway through the book – make us feel something for your characters.

Humor is encouraged. In fact, if you can make us laugh out loud more than once, you'll earn huge bonus points! But that doesn't mean we don't enjoy a good cry, too. Learn more at www.taketwopublishing.com/submission-guidelines.

Made in the USA
Columbia, SC
19 June 2019